The Wind in the Willows
by Kenneth Grahame
Illustrated by Eric Kincaid

Published by Brimax,
A division of Autumn Publishing Limited
©2004 Autumn Publishing Limited
Appledram Barns, Chichester PO20 7EQ

Printed in China

My Little
Wind in the
Willows
Treasury

With the aim of reaching
a wider range of readers,
Kenneth Grahame's text has been
abridged. Some of the most
difficult words have been
simplified and the longer
sentences split for ease of reading
and understanding. Some
chapters from the original edition
have been omitted.

CHAPTER 1

The River Bank

THE Mole had been working very hard all
the morning, spring-cleaning his little home.
First with brooms, then with dusters; then
on ladders and steps and chairs, with a brush
and a pail of whitewash; till he had dust in his
throat and eyes, and splashes of whitewash
all over his black fur, and an aching back
and weary arms. Spring was moving in the
air above and in the earth below and around
him, penetrating even his dark and lowly little
house. It was small wonder, then, that he
suddenly flung down his brush on the floor, said, 'Bother!' and, 'O blow!'
and also, 'Hang spring-cleaning!' and bolted out of the house without even

waiting to put on his coat. Something up above seemed to be calling him and he made for his steep little tunnel. He scraped and scratched and scrabbled and scrooged, and then he scrooged again and scrabbled and scratched and scraped, working busily with his little paws and muttering to himself, 'Up we go! Up we go!' till at last, *pop!* his snout came out into the sunlight, and he found himself rolling in the warm grass of a great meadow. 'This is fine!' he said to himself. 'This is better than whitewashing!' The sunshine struck hot on his fur, soft breezes caressed his heated brow, and after the peace of the underground home he had lived in so long the carol of happy birds fell on his dulled hearing almost like a shout. Jumping off all his four legs at once, in the joy of living and the delight of spring without its cleaning, he went on his way across the meadow till he reached the hedge on the further side.

Hither and thither through the meadows he rambled busily, along the hedgerows, across the copses, finding everywhere birds building, flowers budding, leaves thrusting – everything happy, and progressive, and occupied. And instead of having an uneasy conscience pricking him and whispering 'Whitewash!' he somehow could only feel how jolly it was to be the only idle dog among all these busy citizens. After all, the best part of a holiday is perhaps not so much to be resting yourself, as to see all the other fellows busy working.

He thought his happiness was complete when, as he wandered aimlessly along, suddenly he stood by the edge of a full-fed river. Never in his life had he seen a river before – this sleek, twisting, powerful animal, chasing and chuckling, gripping things with a gurgle and leaving them with a laugh, to fling itself on fresh playmates that shook themselves free, and were caught and held again. All was a-shake and a-shiver – glints and gleams and sparkles, rustle and swirl, chatter and bubble. The Mole was bewitched, entranced, fascinated. By the side of the river he trotted; and tired at last, he sat on the bank, while the river chattered on.

As he sat on the grass and looked across the river, a dark hole in the bank opposite, just above the water's edge, caught his eye, and dreamily he fell to considering what a nice snug dwelling-place it would make for an animal with few wants and fond of a riverside residence, above flood level and away from noise and dust. As he gazed, something bright and small seemed to twinkle down in the heart of it, vanished, then twinkled once more like a tiny star. But it could hardly be a star in such an unlikely situation; and it was too glittering and small for a glow-worm. Then, as he looked, it winked at him, and so declared itself to be an eye; and a small face began gradually to grow up round it, like a frame round a picture.

A brown little face, with whiskers.

A grave round face, with the same twinkle in its eye that had first attracted his notice.

Small neat ears and thick silky hair.

It was the Water Rat!

Then the two animals stood and regarded each other cautiously.

'Hullo, Mole!' said the Water Rat.

'Hullo, Rat!' said the Mole.

'Would you like to come over?' asked the Rat presently.

'Oh, it's all very well to *talk*,' said the Mole, rather crossly, he being new to a river and riverside life and its ways.

The Rat said nothing, but stooped and unfastened a rope and hauled on it; then lightly stepped into a little boat which the Mole had not observed. It was painted blue outside and white within, and was just the size for two animals; and the Mole's whole heart went out to it at once, even though he did not yet fully understand its uses.

The Rat sculled smartly across and made fast. Then he held up his forepaw as the Mole stepped gingerly down. 'Lean on that!' he said. 'Now then, step lively!' and the Mole to his surprise and rapture found himself actually seated in the stern of a real boat.

'This has been a wonderful day!' said he, as the Rat shoved off and took to the sculls again. 'Do you know, I've never been in a boat before in all my life.'

'What?' cried the Rat, open mouthed. 'Never been in a – you never – well, I – what have you been doing, then?'

'Is it so nice as all that?' asked the Mole shyly, though he was quite prepared to believe it as he leant back in his seat and looked at the cushions, the oars, the rowlocks, and all the fascinating fittings, and felt the boat sway lightly under him.

'Nice? It's the *only* thing,' said the Water Rat solemnly, as he leant forward for his stroke. 'Believe me, my young friend, there is *nothing* – absolutely nothing – half so much worth doing as simply messing about in boats. Simply messing,' he went on dreamily: 'messing-about-in-boats; messing...'

'Look ahead, Rat!' cried the Mole suddenly.

It was too late. The boat struck the bank full tilt. The dreamer, the joyous oarsman, lay on his back at the bottom of the boat, his heels in the air.

'...about in boats, or *with* boats,' the Rat went on, picking himself up with a pleasant laugh. 'In or out of 'em, it doesn't matter. Nothing seems really to matter, that's the charm of it. Whether you get away, or whether you don't; whether you arrive at your destination or whether you reach somewhere else, or whether you never get anywhere at all, you're always busy, and you never do anything in particular; and when you've done it there's always something else to do, and you can do it if you like, but you'd much better not. Look here! If you've really nothing else on hand this morning, supposing we drop down the river together, and have a long day of it?'

The Mole waggled his toes from sheer happiness, spread his chest with a sigh of full contentment, and leaned back blissfully into the soft cushions. *'What* a day I'm having!' he said. 'Let us start at once!'

'Hold hard a minute, then!' said the Rat. He looped the painter through a ring in his landing-stage, climbed up into his hole above, and after a short interval reappeared staggering under a fat, wicker luncheon basket.

'Shove that under your feet,' he said to the Mole, as he passed it down into the boat. Then he untied the painter and took the sculls again.

'What's inside it?' asked the Mole, wriggling with curiosity.

'There's cold chicken inside it,' replied the Rat briefly;
'coldtonguecoldhamcoldbeefpickledgherkinssaladfrenchrolls
cresssandwichespottedmeatgingerbeerlemonadesodawater –'

'O stop, stop,' cried the Mole in ecstasies. 'This is too much!'

'Do you really think so?' inquired the Rat seriously. 'It's only what I always take on these little excursions; and the other animals are always telling me that I'm a mean beast and cut it *very* fine!'

The Mole never heard a word he was saying. Absorbed in the new life he was entering upon, intoxicated with the sparkle, the ripple, the scents and the sounds and the sunlight, he trailed a paw in the water and dreamed long waking dreams. The Water Rat, like the good little fellow he was, sculled steadily on and did not disturb him.

'I like your clothes awfully, old chap,' he remarked after some half an hour or so had passed. 'I'm going to get a black velvet smoking-suit myself some day, as soon as I can afford it.'

'I beg your pardon,' said the Mole, pulling himself together with an effort. 'You must think me very rude; but all this is so new to me. So–this–is–a–River!'

'*The* River,' corrected the Rat.

'And you really live by the river? What a jolly life!'

'By it and with it and on it and in it,' said the Rat. 'It's brother and sister to me, and aunts, and company, and food and drink, and (naturally) washing. It's my world, and I don't want any other. What it hasn't got is not worth having, and what it doesn't know is not worth knowing. Lord! The times we've had together! Whether in winter or summer, spring or autumn, it's always got its fun and its excitements. When the floods are on in February, and my cellars and basement are brimming with drink that's no good to me, and the brown water runs by my best bedroom window; or again when it all drops away and shows patches of mud that smells like plum cake, and the rushes and weed clog the channels, and I can potter about dry shod over most of the bed of it and find fresh food to eat, and things careless people have dropped out of boats!'

'But isn't it a bit dull at times?' the Mole ventured to ask. 'Just you and the river, and no one else to pass a word with?'

'No one else to – well, I mustn't be hard on you,' said the Rat patiently. 'You're new to it, and of course you don't know. The bank is so crowded nowadays that many people are moving away altogether. O no, it isn't what it used to be, at all. Otters, kingfishers, dabchicks, moorhens, all of them about all day long and always wanting you to *do* something – as if a fellow had no business of his own to attend to!'

'What lies over *there*?' asked the Mole, waving a paw towards a background of woodland that darkly framed the water-meadows on one side of the river.

'That? O, that's just the Wild Wood,' said the Rat shortly. 'We don't go there very much, we river bankers.'

'Aren't they – aren't they very *nice* people in there?' said the Mole a trifle nervously.

'W-e-ll,' replied the Rat, 'let me see. The squirrels are all right. *And* the rabbits, some of 'em, but rabbits are a mixed lot. And then there's Badger, of course. He lives right in the heart of it; wouldn't live anywhere else, either, if you paid him to do it. Dear old Badger! Nobody interferes with *him*. They'd better not,' he added significantly.

'Why, who *should* interfere with him?' asked the Mole.

'Well, of course there are others,' explained the Rat in a hesitating sort of way. 'Weasels and stoats and foxes and so on. They're all right in a way – I'm very good friends with them – pass the time of day when we meet, and all that – but they break out sometimes, there's no denying it, and then – well, you can't really trust them, and that's the fact.'

'And beyond the Wild Wood again?' Mole asked. 'Where it's all blue and dim, and one sees what may be hills or perhaps they mayn't, and something like the smoke of towns, or is it only cloud drift?'

'Beyond the Wild Wood comes the Wide World,' said the Rat. 'And that's something that doesn't matter, either to you or me. I've never been there, and I'm never going, nor you either, if you've got any sense at all. Don't ever refer to it again, please. Now then! Here's our backwater at last, where we're going to lunch.'

Leaving the main stream, they now passed into what seemed at first sight like a little landlocked lake. Green turf sloped down to either edge, brown snaky tree roots gleamed below the surface of the quiet water. Ahead of them the foamy tumble of a weir, arm-in-arm with a restless dripping mill wheel, that held up a grey gabled mill house, filled the air with a soothing murmur of sound. It was so very beautiful that the Mole could only hold up both forepaws and gasp, 'O my! O my! O my!'

The Rat brought the boat alongside the bank, made her fast, helped the Mole safely ashore, and swung out the luncheon basket. The Mole begged as a favour to be allowed to unpack it all by himself; and the Rat was very pleased to indulge him, and to sprawl at full length on the grass and rest, while his excited friend shook out the tablecloth and spread it, took out all the mysterious packets one by one and arranged their contents in due order, still gasping, 'O my! O my!' at each fresh revelation. When all was ready, the Rat said, 'Now, pitch in, old fellow!' and the Mole was indeed very glad to obey, for he had started his spring-cleaning at a very early hour that morning, as people *will* do, and had not paused for food or drink; and he had been through a very great deal since that distant time which now seemed so many days ago.

'What are you looking at?' said the Rat presently, when the edge of their hunger was somewhat dulled, and the Mole's eyes were able to wander off the tablecloth a little.

'I am looking,' said the Mole, 'at a streak of bubbles that I see travelling along the surface of the water. That is a thing that strikes me as funny.'

'Bubbles? Oho!' said the Rat, and chirruped cheerily in an inviting sort of way.

A broad glistening muzzle showed itself above the edge of the bank, and the Otter hauled himself out and shook the water from his coat.

'Greedy beggars!' he observed, making for the food. 'Why didn't you invite me, Ratty?'

'This was an unplanned affair,' explained the Rat. 'By the way, my friend, Mr Mole.'

'Proud, I'm sure,' said the Otter, and the two animals were friends forthwith.

'Such a rumpus everywhere!' continued the Otter. 'All the world seems out on the river today. I came up this backwater to try and get a moment's peace, and then stumble upon you fellows! At least, I beg pardon, I don't exactly mean that, you know.'

There was a rustle behind them, coming from a hedge wherein last year's leaves still clung thick, and a stripy head, with high shoulders behind it, peered forth on them.

'Come on, old Badger!' shouted the Rat.

The Badger trotted forward a pace or two; then grunted, 'Hm! Company,' and turned his back and disappeared from view.

'That's *just* the sort of fellow he is!' observed the disappointed Rat. 'Simply hates Society! Now we shan't see any more of him today. Well, tell us, *who's* out on the river?'

'Toad's out, for one,' replied the Otter. 'In his brand new wager-boat; new togs, new everything!'

The two animals looked at each other and laughed.

'Once it was nothing but sailing,' said the Rat. 'Then he tired of that and took to punting. Nothing would please him but to punt all day and every day, and a nice mess he made of it. Last year it was house-boating, and we all had to go and stay with him in his house-boat, and pretend we liked it. He was going to spend the rest of his life in a house-boat. It's all the same, whatever he takes up;

he gets tired of it, and starts on something fresh.'

'Such a good fellow, too,' remarked the Otter reflectively. 'But no stability, especially in a boat!'

From where they sat they could get a glimpse of the main stream across the island that separated them; and just then a wager-boat flashed into view, the rower – a short, stout figure – splashing badly and rolling a good deal, but working his hardest. The Rat stood up and hailed him, but Toad, for it was he, shook his head and settled sternly to his work.

'He'll be out of the boat in a minute if he rolls like that,' said the Rat, sitting down again.

'Of course he will,' chuckled the Otter. 'Did I ever tell you that good story about Toad and the lock-keeper? It happened this way. Toad...'

A mayfly swerved unsteadily across the current. A swirl of water and a 'cloop!' and the mayfly was visible no more.

Neither was the Otter.

The Mole looked down. The voice was still in his ears, but the turf whereon he had sprawled was clearly vacant. Not an Otter to be seen, as far as the distant horizon.

But again there was a streak of bubbles on the surface of the river.

The Rat hummed a tune, and the Mole remembered it was not polite to make any sort of comment on the sudden disappearance of one's friends at any moment, for any reason or no reason whatever.

'Well, well,' said the Rat, 'I suppose we ought to be moving. I wonder which of us had better pack the luncheon basket?' He did not speak as if he was frightfully eager for the treat.

'O, please let me,' said the Mole. So, of course, the Rat let him.

Packing the basket was not quite such pleasant work as unpacking the basket. It never is. But the Mole was bent on enjoying everything, and although just when he had got the basket packed and strapped up tightly he saw a plate staring up at him from the grass, and when the job had been done again the Rat pointed out a fork which anybody ought to have seen, and last of all, behold! the mustard pot, which he had been sitting on without knowing it, still, somehow the thing got finished at last, without much loss of temper.

The afternoon sun was getting low as the Rat sculled gently homewards in a dreamy mood, murmuring poetry things over to himself, and not paying much attention to Mole. But the Mole was very full of lunch, and self-satisfaction, and already quite at home in a boat (so he thought) and was getting a bit restless besides: and presently he said, 'Ratty! Please, I want to row, now!'

The Rat shook his head with a smile. 'Not yet, my young friend,' he said, 'wait till you've had a few lessons. It's not so easy as it looks.'

The Mole was quiet for a minute or two. But he began to feel more and more jealous of Rat, sculling so strongly and so easily along, and his pride began to whisper that he could do it every bit as well. He jumped up and seized the sculls, so suddenly that the Rat, who was gazing out over the water and saying more poetry things to himself, was taken by surprise and fell backwards off his seat with his legs in the air for the second time, while the triumphant Mole took his place and grabbed the sculls with entire confidence.

'Stop it, you *silly* fool!' cried the Rat, from the bottom of the boat. 'You can't do it! You'll have us over!'

The Mole flung his sculls back with a flourish, and made a great dig at the water. He missed the surface altogether, his legs flew up above his head, and he found himself lying on the top of the helpless Rat. Greatly alarmed, he made a grab at the side of the boat, and the next moment – Sploosh!

Over went the boat, and he found himself struggling in the river.

O my, how cold the water was, and O, how *very* wet it felt. How it sang in his ears as he went down, down, down! How bright and welcome the sun looked as he rose to the surface coughing and spluttering! How black was his despair when he felt himself sinking again! Then a firm paw gripped him by the back of his neck. It was the Rat, and he was evidently laughing.

The Rat got hold of a scull and shoved it under the Mole's arm; then he did the same by the other side of him and, swimming behind, propelled the poor animal to shore, hauled him out, and set him down on the bank, a squashy, pulpy lump of misery.

When the Rat had rubbed him down a bit, and wrung some of the wet out of him, he said, 'Now then, old fellow! Trot up and down the towing path as hard as you can, till you're warm and dry again, while I dive for the luncheon basket.'

So the dismal Mole, wet on the outside and ashamed on the inside, trotted about till he was fairly dry, while the Rat plunged into the water again, recovered the boat, righted her and made her fast, fetched his floating property to shore and finally dived successfully for the luncheon basket and struggled to land with it.

When all was ready for a start once more, the Mole, limp and dejected, took his seat in the stern of the boat; and as they set off, he said in a low voice, broken with emotion, 'Ratty, my generous friend! I am very sorry indeed for my foolish and ungrateful conduct. My heart quite fails me when I think how I might have lost that beautiful luncheon basket. Indeed, I have been a complete fool, and I know it. Will you overlook it this once and forgive me, and let things go on as before?'

'That's all right, bless you!' responded the Rat cheerily. 'What's a little wet to a Water Rat! I'm more in the water than out of it most days. Don't you think any more about it; and, look here! I really think you had better come and stop with me for a little time. It's very plain and rough, you know – not like Toad's house at all, but you haven't seen that yet; still, I can make you comfortable. And I'll teach you to row, and to swim, and you'll soon be as handy on the water as any of us.'

The Mole was so touched by his kind manner of speaking that he could find no voice to answer him; and he had to brush away a tear or two with the back of his paw. But the Rat kindly looked in another direction, and presently the Mole's spirits revived again, and he was even able to give some straight back-talk to a couple of moorhens who were sniggering to each other about his bedraggled appearance.

When they got home, the Rat made a bright fire in the parlour, and planted the Mole in an armchair in front of it, having fetched down a dressing gown and slippers for him, and told him river stories till supper time. Very thrilling stories they were, too, to an earth dwelling animal like Mole. Stories about weirs, and sudden floods, and leaping pike, and about herons, and how particular they were whom they spoke to; and about adventures down drains, and night fishings with Otter, or excursions far afield with Badger. Supper was a most cheerful meal; but very shortly afterwards a terribly sleepy Mole had to be escorted upstairs by his considerate host, to the best bedroom, where he soon laid his head on his pillow in great peace and contentment, knowing that his new-found friend the River was lapping the sill of his window.

This day was only the first of many similar ones for the Mole, each of them longer and fuller of interest as the ripening summer moved onward. He learnt to swim and to row, and entered into the joy of running water; and with his ear to the reed-stems he caught, at intervals, something of what the wind was whispering so constantly among them.

CHAPTER 2

The Open Road

'RATTY', said the Mole suddenly, one bright summer morning, 'if you please, I want to ask you a favour.'

The Rat was sitting on the river bank, singing a little song. He had just composed it himself, so he was very taken up with it, and would not pay proper attention to Mole or anything else. Since early morning he had been swimming in the river, in company with his friends the ducks. And when the ducks stood on their heads suddenly, as ducks will, he would dive down and tickle their necks, just under where their chins would be if ducks had chins, till they were forced to come to the surface again in a hurry, spluttering and angry and shaking their feathers at him, for it is impossible to say quite *all* you feel when your head is under water. At last they implored him to go away and attend to his own affairs and leave them to mind theirs. So the Rat went away, and sat on the river bank in the sun, and made up a song about them, which he called:

'DUCKS' DITTY'

All along the backwater,
Through the rushes tall,
Ducks are a-dabbling,
Up tails all!

Ducks' tails, drakes' tails,
Yellow feet a-quiver,
Yellow bills all out of sight
Busy in the river!

Slushy green undergrowth
Where the roach swim –
Here we keep our larder,
Cool and full and dim.

Everyone for what he likes!
We like to be
Heads down, tails up,
Dabbling free!

High in the blue above
Swifts whirl and call –
We are down a-dabbling,
Up tails all!

'I don't know that I think so *very* much of that little song, Rat,' observed the Mole cautiously.

'Neither do the ducks,' replied the Rat cheerfully. 'They say, "*Why* can't fellows be allowed to do what they like *when* they like and *as* they like, instead of other fellows sitting on banks and watching them all the time and making remarks and poetry and things about them? What *nonsense* it all is!" That's what the ducks say.'

'So it is, so it is,' said the Mole, with great heartiness.

'No, it isn't!' cried the Rat indignantly.

'Well then, it isn't, it isn't,' replied the Mole soothingly. 'But what I wanted to ask you was, won't you take me to call on Mr Toad? I've heard so much about him, and I do so want to make his acquaintance.'

'Why, certainly,' said the good-natured Rat, jumping to his feet and dismissing poetry from his mind for the day. 'Get the boat out, and we'll paddle up there at once. It's never the wrong time to call on Toad. Early or late, he's always the same fellow. Always good-tempered, always glad to see you, always sorry when you go!'

'He must be a very nice animal,' observed the Mole, as he got into the

boat and took the sculls, while the Rat settled himself comfortably in the stern.

'He is indeed the best of animals,' replied Rat. 'So simple, so good-natured, and so affectionate. Perhaps he's not very clever – we can't all be geniuses; and it may be that he is both boastful and conceited. But he has got some great qualities, has Toady.'

Rounding a bend in the river, they came in sight of a handsome, dignified old house of mellowed red brick, with well-kept lawns reaching down to the water's edge.

'There's Toad Hall,' said the Rat, 'and that creek on the left, where the notice-board says "Private. No landing allowed", leads to his boat-house, where we'll leave the boat. The stables are over there to the right. That's the banqueting hall you're looking at now – very old, that is. Toad is rather rich, you know, and this is really one of the nicest houses in these parts, though we never admit as much to Toad.'

They glided up the creek, and passed into the shadow of a large boat-house. Here they saw many handsome boats, slung from the cross-beams or hauled up on a slip, but none in the water; and the place had an unused and a deserted air.

The Rat looked around him. 'I understand,' said he. 'Boating is played out. He's tired of it, and done with it. I wonder what new fad he has taken up now? Come along and let's look him up. We shall hear all about it quite soon enough.'

They disembarked, and strolled across the gay flower-decked lawns in search of Toad, whom they soon saw resting in a wicker garden chair, with a preoccupied expression on his face, and a large map spread out on his knees.

'Hooray!' he cried, jumping up on seeing them, 'this is splendid!' He shook the paws of both of them warmly, never waiting for an introduction to the Mole. 'How *kind* of you!' he went on, dancing round them. 'I was just going to send a boat down the river for you, Ratty, with strict orders that you were to be fetched up here at once, whatever you were doing. I want you badly, both of you. Now what will you take? Come inside and have something! You don't know how lucky it is, your turning up just now!'

'Let's sit quiet a bit, Toady!' said the Rat, throwing himself into an easy chair, while the Mole took another by the side of him and made some civil remark about Toad's 'delightful residence'.

'Finest house on the whole river,' cried Toad boisterously. 'Or anywhere else, for that matter,' he could not help adding.

Here the Rat nudged the Mole. Unfortunately the Toad saw him do it, and turned very red. There was a moment's painful silence. Then Toad burst out laughing. 'All right, Ratty,' he said. 'It's only my way, you know. And it's not such a very bad house, is it? You know you rather like it yourself. Now, look here. Let's be sensible. You are the very animals I wanted. You've got to help me. It's most important!'

'It's about your rowing, I suppose,' said the Rat, with an innocent air. 'You're getting on fairly well, though you splash a good bit still. With a great deal of patience, and a certain amount of coaching, you may –'.

'O, pooh! Boating!' interrupted the Toad, in great disgust. 'Silly boyish amusement. I've given that up *long* ago. Sheer waste of time, that's what it is. It makes me downright sorry to see you fellows, who ought to know better, spending all your energies in that aimless manner. No, I've discovered the real thing, the only genuine occupation for a lifetime. I propose to devote the remainder of mine to it, and can only regret the wasted years that lie behind me, squandered in trivialities. Come with me, dear Ratty, and your amiable friend also, if he will be so very good, just as far as the stable yard, and you shall see what you shall see!'

He led the way to the stable yard, the Rat following with a most mistrustful expression; and there, drawn out of the coach-house into the open, they saw a gipsy caravan, shining with newness, painted a canary-yellow picked out with green, with red wheels.

'There you are!' cried the Toad, standing before them legs apart, chest

out. 'There's real life for you, embodied in that little cart. The open road, the dusty highway, the heath, the common, the hedgerows, the rolling downs! Camps, villages, towns, cities! Here today, up and off to somewhere else tomorrow! Travel, change, interest, excitement! The whole world before you, and a horizon that's always changing! And mind, this is the very finest cart of its sort that was ever built, without any exception. Come inside and look. Planned it all myself, I did!'

The Mole was tremendously interested and excited, and followed him eagerly up the steps and into the caravan. The Rat only snorted and thrust his hands deep into his pockets, remaining where he was.

It was indeed very compact and comfortable. Little sleeping-bunks, a little table that folded up against the wall, a cooking stove, lockers, bookshelves, a bird cage with a bird in it; and pots, pans, jugs and kettles of every size and variety.

'All complete!' said the Toad triumphantly, pulling open a locker. 'You see, biscuits, potted lobster, sardines – everything you can possibly want. Soda water here, tobacco there, letter-paper, bacon, jam, cards and dominoes – you'll find,' he continued, as they descended the steps again, 'you'll find that nothing whatever has been forgotten, when we make our start this afternoon.'

'I beg your pardon,' said the Rat slowly, as he chewed a straw, 'but did I overhear you say something about "*we*", and "*start*", and "*this afternoon*"?'

'Now, you dear good old Ratty,' said Toad imploringly, 'don't begin talking in that stiff and sniffy sort of way, because you know you've *got* to come. I can't possibly manage without you, so please consider it settled, and don't argue, it's the one thing I can't stand. You surely don't mean to stick to your dull smelly old river all your life, and just live in a hole in a bank, and *boat*? I want to show you the world! I'm going to make an *animal* of you, my boy!'

'I don't care,' said the Rat doggedly. 'I'm not coming, and that's flat. And I *am* going to stick to my old river, *and* live in a hole, *and* boat, as I've always done. And what's more, Mole's going to stick to me and do as I do, aren't you, Mole?'

'Of course I am,' said the Mole loyally. 'I'll always stick to you, Rat, and what you say is to be has got to be. All the same, it sounds as if it might have been well, rather fun, you know!' he added wistfully. Poor Mole! The Life Adventurous was so new a thing to him and so thrilling; and this fresh aspect of it was so tempting; and he had fallen in love at first sight with the canary coloured cart and all its little fitments.

The Rat saw what was passing in his mind, and wavered. He hated disappointing people, and he was fond of the Mole, and would do almost anything to oblige him. Toad was watching both of them closely.

'Come along in and have some lunch,' he said diplomatically, 'and we'll talk it over. We needn't decide anything in a hurry. Of course, I don't really care. I only want to give pleasure to you fellows. "Live for others!" That's my motto in life.'

During lunch – which was excellent, of course, as everything at Toad Hall always was, the Toad simply let himself go. Ignoring the Rat, he painted the prospects of the trip and the joys of the open life and the roadside in such glowing colours that the Mole could hardly sit in his chair for excitement. Somehow, it soon seemed taken for granted by all three of them that the trip was a settled thing; and the Rat, though still unconvinced in his mind, allowed his good nature to override his personal objections. He could not bear to disappoint his two friends, who were already planning out each day's separate occupation for several weeks ahead.

When they were quite ready, the now triumphant Toad led his companions to the paddock and set them to capture the old grey horse, who, without having been consulted, and to his own extreme annoyance, had been chosen by Toad for the dustiest job in this dusty expedition. He frankly preferred the paddock, and took a deal of catching. Meantime Toad packed the lockers still tighter with necessaries, and hung nosebags, nets of onions, bundles of hay, and baskets from the bottom of the cart. At last the horse was caught and harnessed, and they set off, all talking at once, each animal either trudging by the side of the cart or sitting on the shaft, as the mood took him. It was a golden afternoon. The smell of the dust they kicked up was rich and satisfying; out of thick

orchards on either side of the road, birds called and whistled to them cheerily; good-natured wayfarers, passing them, gave them 'Good day', or stopped to say nice things about their beautiful cart; and rabbits, sitting at their front doors in the hedgerows, held up their forepaws, and said, 'O my! O my! O my!'

Late in the evening, tired and happy and miles from home, they drew up on a remote common far from any houses, turned the horse loose to graze, and ate their simple supper sitting on the grass by the side of the cart. Toad talked big about all he was going to do in the days to come, while stars grew fuller and larger all around them, and a yellow moon, appearing suddenly and silently from nowhere in particular, came to keep them company and listen to their talk. At last they turned into their little bunks in the cart; and Toad, kicking out his legs, sleepily said, 'Well, good night, you fellows! This is the real life for a gentleman! Talk about your old river!'

'I *don't* talk about my river,' replied the patient Rat. 'You *know* I don't, Toad. But I *think* about it,' he added pathetically, in a lower tone: 'I think about it all the time!'

The Mole reached out from under his blanket, felt for the Rat's paw in the darkness, and gave it a squeeze. 'I'll do whatever you like, Ratty,' he whispered. 'Shall we run away tomorrow morning, quite early – *very* early – and go back to our dear old hole on the river?'

'No, no, we'll see it out,' whispered back the Rat. 'Thanks awfully, but I ought to stick by Toad till this trip is ended. It wouldn't be safe for him to be left to himself. It won't take very long. His fads never do. Good night!'

The end was indeed nearer than even the Rat suspected.

After so much open air and excitement the Toad slept very soundly, and no amount of shaking could rouse him out of bed next morning. So the Mole and Rat set to work, quietly and manfully, and while the Rat saw to the horse, and lit a fire, and cleaned last night's cups and plates, and got things ready for breakfast, the Mole trudged off to the nearest village, a long way off, for milk and eggs and various necessaries the Toad had, of course, forgotten to provide. The hard work had all been done, and the two animals were resting, thoroughly exhausted, by the time Toad appeared on the scene, fresh and gay, remarking what a pleasant easy life it was they were all leading now, after the cares and worries of house-keeping at home.

They had a pleasant ramble that day over grassy downs and along narrow by-lanes, and camped, as before, on a common, only this time the two guests took care that Toad should do his fair share of work. In consequence, when the time came for starting next morning, Toad was by no means so happy about the simplicity of the primitive life, and indeed attempted to resume his place in his bunk, from where he was hauled by force. Their way lay, as before, across country by narrow lanes, and it was not till the afternoon that they came out on the high road, their first high road; and there disaster, sudden and unexpected, sprang out on them – disaster that was momentous indeed to their expedition, but simply overwhelming in its effect on the future career of Toad.

They were strolling along the high road easily, the Mole by the horse's head, talking to him, since the horse had complained that he was being frightfully left out of it, and nobody considered him in the least; the Toad and the Water Rat walking behind the cart talking together – at least, Toad was talking, and Rat was saying at intervals, 'Yes, precisely; and what did *you* say to *him*?' and thinking all the time of something very different, when far behind them they heard a faint warning hum, like the drone of a distant bee. Glancing back, they saw a small cloud of dust, with a dark centre, advancing on them at incredible speed, while from out of the dust a faint 'Poop-poop!' wailed like an uneasy animal in pain. Hardly regarding it, they turned to resume their conversation, when in an instant (as it seemed) the peaceful scene was changed, and with a blast of wind and a whirl of sound that made them jump for the nearest ditch, it was on them! The 'poop-poop' rang with a blaring shout in their ears, they had a moment's glimpse of an interior of glittering plate-glass and rich leather, and the magnificent motor-car, immense, breath-snatching, passionate, with its driver tense and hugging his wheel, claimed all earth and air for a fraction of a second. It flung a cloud of dust that blinded and enwrapped them utterly, and then dwindled to a speck in the far distance, and changed back into a droning bee once more.

The old grey horse, dreaming, as he plodded along, of his quiet paddock, in a new situation such as this simply abandoned himself to his natural emotions. Rearing, plunging, backing steadily, in spite of all the Mole's efforts at his head, and all the Mole's lively language appealing to his better nature, he drove the cart backwards towards the deep ditch at the side of the road. It wavered an instant, then there was a heartrending crash, and the canary coloured cart, their pride and their joy, lay on its side in the ditch, a complete wreck.

The Rat danced up and down in the road, simply transported with passion. 'You villains!' he shouted, shaking both fists. 'You scoundrels, you highwaymen, you – you – road-hogs! I'll have the law on you! I'll report you! I'll take you through all the Courts!' His home-sickness had quite slipped away from him.

Toad sat straight down in the middle of the dusty road, his legs stretched out before him, and stared fixedly in the direction of the disappearing motor-car. His face wore a placid, satisfied expression, and at intervals he faintly murmured, 'Poop-poop!'

The Mole was busy trying to quiet the horse, which he succeeded in doing after a time. Then he went to look at the cart, on its side in the ditch. It was indeed a sorry sight. Panels and windows smashed, axles hopelessly bent, one wheel off, sardine tins scattered over the wide world, and the bird in the bird cage sobbing pitifully and calling to be let out.

The Rat came to help him, but their united efforts were not sufficient to right the cart. 'Hi! Toad!' they cried. 'Come and bear a hand, can't you?'

The Toad never answered a word, or budged from his seat in the road; so they went to see what was the matter with him. They found him in a sort of trance, a happy smile on his face, his eyes still fixed on the dusty wake of their destroyer. At intervals he was still heard to murmur, 'Poop-poop!'

The Rat shook him by the shoulder. 'Are you coming to help us, Toad?' he demanded sternly.

'Glorious, stirring sight!' murmured Toad, never offering to move. 'The poetry of motion! The *real* way to travel! The *only* way to travel! Here today – in next week tomorrow! Villages skipped, towns and cities jumped! O bliss! O poop-poop! O my! O my!'

'O *stop* being a fool, Toad!' cried the Mole despairingly.

'And to think I never *knew*!' the Toad went on. 'All those wasted years that lie behind me, I never knew, never even *dreamt*! But *now*, but now that I know, now that I fully realise! O what a flowery track lies spread before me now! What dust clouds shall spring up behind me as I speed on my reckless way! What carts I shall fling carelessly into the ditch in the wake of my magnificent charge! Horrid little carts, common carts, canary coloured carts!'

'What are we to do with him?' asked the Mole of the Water Rat.

'Nothing at all,' replied the Rat firmly. 'Because there is really nothing to be done. You see, I know him of old. He is now possessed. He has got a new craze, and it always takes him that way, in its first stage. He'll continue like that for days now, like an animal walking in a happy dream. Never mind him. Let's go and see what there is to be done about the cart.'

A careful inspection showed them that, even if they succeeded in righting it by themselves, the cart would travel no longer. The axles were in a hopeless state, and the missing wheel was shattered into pieces.

The Rat knotted the horse's reins over his back and took him by the head, carrying the bird cage in the other hand.

'Come on!' he said grimly to the Mole. 'It's five or six miles to the nearest town, and we shall just have to walk it. The sooner we make a start the better.'

'But what about Toad?' asked the Mole anxiously, as they set off together. 'We can't leave him here, sitting in the middle of the road by himself, in the state he's in! It's not safe. Supposing another Thing were to come along?'

'O, *bother* Toad,' said the Rat savagely; 'I've done with him!'

They had not proceeded very far on their way, however, when there was a pattering of feet behind them, and Toad caught them up and thrust a paw inside the elbow of each of them; still breathing short and staring into vacancy.

'Now, look here, Toad!' said the Rat sharply. 'As soon as we get to the town, you'll have to go straight to the police station, and see if they know anything about that motor-car and who it belongs to, and lodge a complaint against it. And then you'll have to go to a blacksmith's or a wheelwright's and arrange for the cart to be fetched and mended and put to rights. It'll take time, but it's not quite a hopeless smash. Meanwhile, the Mole and I will go to an inn and find comfortable rooms where we can stay till the cart's ready, and till your nerves have recovered from their shock.'

'Police station! Complaint!' murmured Toad dreamily. 'Me *complain* of that beautiful, that heavenly vision! *Mend* the *cart*! I've done with carts for ever. I never want to see the cart, or to hear of it again. O Ratty! You can't think how obliged I am to you for consenting to come on this trip! I wouldn't have gone without you, and then I might never have seen that, that swan, that sunbeam, that thunderbolt! I might never have heard that entrancing sound, or smelt that bewitching smell! I owe it all to you, my best of friends!'

The Rat turned from him in despair. 'You see what it is?' he said to the Mole, addressing him across Toad's head. 'He's quite hopeless. I give it up: when we get to the town we'll go to the railway station, and with luck we may pick up a train there that'll get us back to River Bank tonight. And if ever you catch me going out with this provoking animal again...' He snorted, and during the rest of that weary trudge addressed his remarks exclusively to Mole.

On reaching the town they went straight to the station and deposited Toad in the second-class waiting room, giving a porter twopence to keep a strict eye on him. They then left the horse at an inn stable, and gave what directions they could about the cart and its contents. Eventually, a slow train having landed them at a station not very far from Toad Hall, they escorted the spellbound, sleep-walking Toad to his door, put him inside it, and instructed his housekeeper to feed him, undress him, and put him to bed.

Then they got out their boat from the boat house, sculled down the river, and at a very late hour sat down to supper in their own snug little riverside parlour, to the Rat's great joy and contentment.

The following evening the Mole, who had got up late and taken things very easy all day, was sitting on the bank fishing, when the Rat, who had been looking up his friends and gossiping, came strolling along to find him. 'Heard the news?' he said. 'There's nothing else being talked about, all along the river bank. Toad went up to Town by an early train this morning. And he has ordered a large and very expensive motor-car.

CHAPTER 3

The Wild Wood

THE Mole had long wanted to meet the Badger.
He seemed, by all accounts, to be such an important
person and, though rarely seen, to have an influence
on everybody about the place. But whenever the Mole
mentioned his wish to the Water Rat he always found
himself put off. 'It's all right', the Rat would say. 'Badger'll
turn up some day or other, he's always turning up, and
then I'll introduce you. The best of fellows! But you must
not only take him *as* you find him, but *when* you find him!'

'Couldn't you ask him here, to dinner or something?'
said the Mole.

'He wouldn't come', replied the Rat simply. 'Badger
hates Society, and invitations, and dinner, and all that
sort of thing.'

'Well, then, supposing we go and call on *him*?' suggested the Mole.

'O, I'm sure he wouldn't like that at *all*,' said the Rat, quite alarmed. 'He's so very shy, he'd be sure to be offended. I've never even ventured to call on him at his own home myself, though I know him so well. Besides, we can't. It's quite out of the question, because he lives in the very middle of the Wild Wood.'

'Well, supposing he does,' said the Mole. 'You told me the Wild Wood was all right, you know.'

'O, I know, I know, so it is,' replied the Rat. 'But I think we won't go there just now. Not *just* yet. It's a long way, and he wouldn't be at home at this time of year anyhow, and he'll be coming along some day, if you'll wait quietly.'

The Mole had to be content with this. But the Badger never came along, and every day brought its amusements, and it was not till summer was long over, and cold and frost kept them much indoors, and the swollen river raced past outside their windows with a speed that made boating impossible, that he found his thoughts dwelling again on the grey Badger, who lived his own life by himself, in his hole in the middle of the Wild Wood.

In the winter time the Rat slept a great deal, retiring early and rising late. During his short day he sometimes scribbled poetry or did other small jobs about the house; and, of course, there were always animals dropping in for a chat, and so there was a good deal of story-telling and comparing notes on the past summer and all its doings.

There was plenty to talk about on those short winter days when the animals found themselves round the fire; still, the Mole had a good deal of spare time on his hands, and so one afternoon, when the Rat in his armchair before the blaze was alternately dozing and trying over rhymes that wouldn't fit, he decided to go out by himself and explore the Wild Wood, and perhaps strike up an acquaintance with Mr Badger.

It was a cold, still afternoon with a hard steely sky overhead, when he slipped out of the warm parlour into the open air. The country lay bare and entirely leafless around him as he pushed on towards the Wild Wood, which lay before him low and threatening, like a black reef in some still southern sea.

There was nothing to alarm him at first. Twigs crackled under his feet, logs tripped him, fungi on stumps looked like faces, and startled him for the moment; but that was all fun, and exciting. It led him on, and he went deeper to where the light was less, and trees crouched nearer and nearer, and holes made ugly mouths at him on either side.

Everything was very still now. The dusk advanced on him steadily, rapidly, gathering in behind and in front; and the light seemed to be draining away like flood water.

Then the faces began.

It was over his shoulder that he first thought he saw a face: a little evil wedge-shaped face, looking out at him from a hole. When he turned and confronted it, the thing had vanished.

He quickened his pace, telling

himself cheerfully not to begin imagining things, or there would be simply no end to it. He passed another hole, and another, and another; and then a little narrow face, with hard eyes, flashed up for an instant from a hole, and was gone. He hesitated, braced himself up for an effort and strode on. Then suddenly, and as if it had been so all the time, every hole, far and near, and there were hundreds of them, seemed to possess its face, coming and going rapidly, all fixing on him glances of malice and hatred: all hard-eyed and evil and sharp.

If he could only get away from the holes in the banks, he thought, there would be no more faces. He swung off the path and plunged into the untrodden places of the wood.

Then the whistling began.

Very faint and shrill it was, and far behind him when first he heard it; but somehow it made him hurry forward. Then, still very faint and shrill, it sounded far ahead of him, and made him hesitate and want to go back. As he halted in indecision it broke out on either side, and seemed to be caught up and passed on throughout the whole length of the wood to its furthest limit. They were up and alert and ready, evidently, whoever they were! And he – he was alone, and unarmed, and far from any help; and the night was closing in.

Then the pattering began.

He thought it was only falling leaves at first, so slight and delicate was the sound of it. Then as it grew it took a regular rhythm, and he knew it for nothing else but the pat-pat-pat of little feet, still a very long way off. Was it in front or behind? It seemed to be first one, then the other, then both. It grew and it multiplied, till from every quarter as he listened anxiously, leaning this way and that, it seemed to be closing in on him.

The pattering increased till it sounded like sudden hail on the dry leaf carpet spread around him. The whole wood seemed to be running now, running hard, hunting, chasing, closing in round something or – somebody. In panic, he began to run too, aimlessly, he knew not where. He ran up against things, he fell over things and into things, he darted under things and dodged round things. At last he took refuge in the dark deep hollow of an old beech tree,

which offered shelter, a hiding place, perhaps even safety, but who could tell? Anyhow, he was too tired to run any further, and could only snuggle down into the dry leaves which had drifted into the hollow, and hope he was safe for the time. And as he lay there panting and trembling, and listened to the whistlings and the patterings outside, he knew it at last, in all its fullness, that dreadful thing which other little dwellers in field and hedgerow had encountered here, and known as their darkest moment; that thing which the Rat had tried to shield him from: the Terror of the Wild Wood!

Meantime the Rat, warm and comfortable, dozed by his fireside. His paper of half-finished verses slipped from his knee, his head fell back, his mouth opened, and he wandered by the grassy banks of dream rivers. Then a coal slipped, the fire crackled and sent up a spurt of flame, and he woke with a start. Remembering what he had been engaged upon, he reached down to the floor for his verses, pored over them for a minute, and then looked round for the Mole to ask him if he knew a good rhyme for something or other.

But the Mole was not there.

He listened for a time. The house seemed very quiet.

Then he called 'Moley!' several times, and, receiving no answer, got up and went out into the hall.

The Mole's cap was missing from its accustomed peg. His boots, which always lay by the umbrella stand, were also gone.

The Rat left the house and carefully examined the muddy surface of the ground outside, hoping to find the Mole's tracks. There they were, sure enough. The boots were new, just bought for the winter, and the pimples on their soles were fresh and sharp. He could see the imprints of them in the mud, running along straight and purposeful, leading direct to the Wild Wood.

The Rat looked very grave, and stood in deep thought for a minute or two. Then he re-entered the house, strapped a belt round his waist, shoved a pair of pistols into it, took up a stout cudgel that stood in a corner of the hall, and set off for the Wild Wood at a smart pace.

It was already getting towards dusk when he reached the first fringe of trees and plunged without hesitation into the wood, looking anxiously on either side for any sign of his friend. Here and there wicked little faces popped out of holes, but vanished immediately at the sight of the brave animal, his pistols, and the great ugly cudgel in his grasp; and the whistling and pattering, which he had heard quite plainly on his first entry, died away and ceased, and all was very still. He made his way manfully through the length of the wood, to its furthest edge; then, forsaking all paths, he set himself to cross it bit by bit, working over the whole ground, and all the time calling out cheerfully, 'Moley, Moley, Moley! Where are you? It's me – it's old Rat!'

He had patiently hunted through the wood for an hour or more, when at last to his joy he heard a little answering cry. Guiding himself by the sound, he made his way through the gathering darkness to the foot of an old beech tree, with a hole in it, and from out of the hole came a feeble voice, saying, 'Ratty! Is that really you?'

The Rat crept into the hollow, and there he found the Mole, exhausted and still trembling. 'O, Rat!' he cried. 'I've been so frightened, you can't think!'

'O, I quite understand,' said the Rat soothingly. 'You shouldn't really have gone and done it, Mole. I did my best to keep you from it. We river-bankers, we hardly ever come here by ourselves. If we have to come, we come in couples, at least; then we're generally all right. Besides, there are a hundred things one has to know, which we understand all about and you don't, as yet. I mean passwords, and signs, and plants you carry in your pocket, and verses you repeat, and dodges and tricks you can use; all simple enough when you know them, but they've got to be known if you're small, or you'll find yourself in trouble. Of course, if you were Badger or Otter, it would be quite another matter.'

'Surely the brave Mr Toad wouldn't mind coming here by himself, would he?' inquired the Mole.

'Old Toad?' said the Rat, laughing heartily. 'He wouldn't show his face here alone, not for a whole hatfull of golden guineas, Toad wouldn't.'

The Mole was greatly cheered by the sound of the Rat's careless laughter, as well as by the sight of his stick and his gleaming pistols, and he stopped shivering and began to feel bolder and more himself again.

'Now then,' said the Rat presently, 'we really must pull ourselves together and make a start for home while there's still a little light left. It will never do to spend the night here, you understand. Too cold, for one thing.'

'Dear Ratty,' said the poor Mole, 'I'm dreadfully sorry, but I'm simply dead beat and that's a fact. You *must* let me rest here a while longer, and get my strength back, if I'm to get home at all.'

'O, all right', said the good-natured Rat, 'rest away. It's pretty nearly pitch dark now, anyhow; and there ought to be a bit of a moon later.'

So the Mole got well into the dry leaves and stretched himself out, and presently dropped off into sleep, though of a broken and troubled sort; while the Rat covered himself up, too, as best he might, for warmth, and lay patiently waiting, with a pistol in his paw.

When at last the Mole woke up, much refreshed and in his usual spirits, the Rat said, 'Now then! I'll just take a look outside and see if everything's quiet, and then we really must be off.'

He went to the entrance of their retreat and put his head out. Then the Mole heard him saying quietly to himself, 'Hullo! Hullo! Here *is* a go!'

'What's up, Ratty?' asked the Mole.

'*Snow* is up', replied the Rat briefly; 'or rather, *down*. It's snowing hard.'

The Mole came and crouched beside him, and, looking out, saw the wood that had been so dreadful to him in quite a changed aspect. Holes, hollows, pools, pitfalls, and other black menaces to the wayfarer were vanishing fast, and a gleaming carpet of snow was springing up everywhere, that looked too delicate to be trodden upon by rough feet. A fine powder filled the air and caressed the cheek with a tingle in its touch, and the black boles of the trees showed up in a light that seemed to come from below.

'Well, well, it can't be helped', said the Rat after pondering. 'We must make a start, and take our chance, I suppose. The worst of it is, I don't exactly know where we are. And now this snow makes everything look so very different.'

It did indeed. The Mole would not have known that it was the same wood. However, they set out bravely, and took the line that seemed most promising, holding on to each other and pretending that they recognised an old friend in every fresh tree that grimly and silently greeted them, or saw openings, gaps, or paths with a familiar turn in them, in the endless scene of white space and black tree trunks that refused to vary.

An hour or two later they pulled up, downhearted, weary, and hopelessly at sea, and sat down on a fallen tree trunk to recover their breath and consider what was to be done. They were aching with fatigue and bruised with tumbles; they had fallen into several holes and got wet through; the snow was getting so deep that they could hardly drag their little legs through it, and the trees were thicker and more like each other than ever. There seemed to be no end to this wood, and no beginning, and no difference in it, and, worst of all, no way out.

'We can't sit here very long,' said the Rat. 'We shall have to make another push for it, and do something or other. The cold is too awful for anything, and the snow will soon be too deep for us to wade through.' He peered about him and considered. 'Look here,' he went on, 'this is what occurs to me. There's a sort of dell down there in front of us, where the ground seems all hilly and humpy and hummocky. We'll make our way down into that, and try and find some sort of shelter, a cave or hole with a dry floor to it, out of the snow and the wind, and there we'll have a good rest before we try again, for we're both of us pretty dead beat. Besides, the snow may leave off, or something may turn up.'

So once more they got on their feet, and struggled down into the dell, where they hunted about for a cave or some corner that was dry and a protection from the bitter wind and the whirling snow. They were investigating one of the hummocky bits the Rat had spoken of, when suddenly the Mole tripped up and fell forward on his face with a squeal.

'O, my leg!' he cried. 'O, my poor shin!' and he sat up on the snow and nursed his leg in both his front paws.

'Poor old Mole!' said the Rat kindly. 'You don't seem to be having much luck today, do you? Let's have a look at the leg. Yes,' he went on, going down on his knees to look, 'you've cut your shin, sure enough. Wait till I get at my handkerchief, and I'll tie it up for you.'

'I must have tripped over a hidden branch or a stump,' said the Mole miserably. 'O my! O my!'

'It's a very clean cut,' said the Rat, examining it again attentively. 'That was never done by a branch or a stump. Looks as if it was made by a sharp edge of something metal. Funny!' He pondered a while, and examined the humps and slopes that surrounded them.

'Well, never mind what done it,' said the Mole, forgetting his grammar in his pain. 'It hurts just the same, whatever done it.'

But the Rat, after carefully tying up the leg with his handkerchief, had left him and was busy scraping in the snow. He scratched and shovelled and explored, all four legs working busily, while the Mole waited impatiently, remarking at intervals, 'O, *come* on, Rat!'

Suddenly the Rat cried, 'Hooray!' and then, 'Hooray-oo-ray-oo-ray-oo-ray!' and danced a feeble jig in the snow.

'What *have* you found, Ratty?' asked the Mole, still nursing his leg.

'Come and see!' said the delighted Rat, as he jigged on.

The Mole hobbled up to the spot and had a good look.

'Well,' he said at last, slowly, 'I *see* it right enough. Seen the same sort of thing before, lots of times. Familiar object, I call it. A door-scraper! Well, what of it? Why dance jigs round a door-scraper?'

'But don't you see what it *means*, you dull-witted animal?' cried the Rat impatiently.

'Of course I see what it means,' replied the Mole. 'It simply means that some *very* careless and forgetful person has left his door-scraper lying about in the middle of the Wild Wood, *just* where it's *sure* to trip *everybody* up. Very thoughtless of him, I call it. When I get home I shall go and complain about it to somebody or other, see if I don't!'

'O dear! O dear!' cried the Rat, in despair. 'Here, stop arguing and come and scrape!' And he set to work again and made the snow fly in all directions around him.

After some further toil his efforts were rewarded, and a very shabby doormat lay exposed to view.

'There, what did I tell you?' exclaimed the Rat in great triumph.

'Absolutely nothing whatever,' replied the Mole, with perfect truthfulness. 'Well now,' he went on, 'you seem to have found another piece of domestic litter, done for and thrown away, and I suppose you're perfectly happy. Better go ahead and dance your jig round that if you've got to, and get it over, and then perhaps we can go on and not waste any more time over rubbish heaps. Can we *eat* a doormat? Or sleep under a doormat? Or sit on a doormat and sledge home over the snow on it, you exasperating rodent?'

'Do you mean to say,' cried the excited Rat, 'that this doormat doesn't *tell* you anything?'

'Really, Rat,' said the Mole quite grumpily, 'I think we've had enough of this folly. Whoever heard of a doormat *telling* anyone anything? They simply don't do it. They are not that sort at all. Doormats know their place.'

'Now look here, you – you thick-headed beast,' replied the Rat, really angry, 'this must stop. Not another word, but scrape – scrape and scratch and dig and hunt around, especially on the sides of the hummocks, if you want to sleep dry and warm tonight, for it's our last chance!'

The Rat attacked a snow-bank beside them with great energy, probing with his cudgel everywhere and then digging with fury; and the Mole scraped busily too, more to oblige the Rat than for any other reason, for his opinion was that his friend was getting light-headed.

Some ten minutes' hard work, and the point of the Rat's cudgel struck something that sounded hollow. He worked till he could get a paw through and feel; then called the Mole to come and help him. Hard at it went the two animals, till at last the result of their labours stood full in view of the astonished Mole.

In the side of what had seemed to be a snow bank stood a solid looking little door, painted a dark green. An iron bell-pull hung by the side, and below it, on a small brass plate, neatly engraved in square capital letters, they could read by the aid of moonlight: MR BADGER

The Mole fell backwards on the snow from sheer surprise and delight. 'Rat!' he cried, 'you're a wonder! A real wonder, that's what you are. I see it all now! You argued it out, step by step, in that wise head of yours, from the very moment that I fell and cut my shin, and you looked at the cut, and at once your majestic mind said to itself, "Door-scraper!" And then you turned to and found the very door-scraper that done it! Did you stop there? No. Some people would have been quite satisfied; but not you. Your intellect went on working. "Let me only just find a doormat," says you to yourself, "and my theory is proved!" And of course you found your doormat. You're so clever, I believe you could find anything you liked. If I only had your head, Ratty'.

'But as you haven't', interrupted the Rat rather unkindly, 'I suppose you're going to sit on the snow all night and *talk*? Get up at once and hang on to that bell-pull you see there, and ring hard, as hard as you can, while I hammer!'

While the Rat attacked the door with his stick, the Mole sprang up at the bell-pull, clutched it and swung there, both feet well off the ground, and from quite a long way off they could faintly hear a deep-toned bell respond.

CHAPTER 4

Mr Badger

THEY waited patiently for what seemed a very long time, stamping in the snow to keep their feet warm. At last they heard the sound of slow shuffling footsteps approaching the door from the inside. It seemed, as the Mole remarked to the Rat, like someone walking in carpet slippers that were too large for him and down-at-heel; which was clever of Mole, because that was exactly what it was.

There was the noise of a bolt shot back, and the door opened a few inches, enough to show a long snout and a pair of sleepy blinking eyes.

'Now, the very next time this happens,' said a gruff voice, 'I shall be exceedingly angry. Who is it *this* time, disturbing people on such a night? Speak up!'

'O, Badger,' cried the Rat, 'let us in, please. It's me, Rat, and my friend Mole, and we've lost our way in the snow.'

'What, Ratty, my dear little man!' exclaimed the Badger, in quite a different voice. 'Come along in, both of you, at once. Why, you must be frozen. Well I never! Lost in the snow! And in the Wild Wood too, and at this time of night! But come in.'

The two animals tumbled over each other in their eagerness to get inside, and with great joy and relief heard the door shut behind them.

The Badger, who wore a long dressing-gown, and whose slippers were indeed very down-at-heel, carried a flat candlestick in his paw and had probably been on his way to bed when he heard their call. He looked kindly down on them and patted both their heads. 'This is not the sort of night for small animals to be out,' he said paternally. 'I'm afraid you've been up to some of your pranks again, Ratty. But come along; come into the kitchen. There's a first-rate fire there, and supper and everything.'

He shuffled on in front of them, carrying the light, and they followed him, nudging each other in an excited sort of way, down a long, gloomy, and to tell the truth, decidedly shabby passage, into a sort of a central hall, out of which they could dimly see other long tunnel-like passages. But there were doors in the hall as well: stout oak doors. One of these the Badger flung open, and at once they found themselves in all the glow and warmth of a large fire-lit kitchen.

The floor was well-worn red brick, and on the wide hearth burnt a fire of logs, between two attractive chimney-corners tucked away in the wall, well out of any draught. A couple of high-backed seats, facing each other on either side of the fire, gave further sitting accommodation. In the middle of the room stood a long table of plain boards placed on trestles, with benches down each side. At one end of it, where an armchair stood pushed back, were spread the remains of the Badger's plain but ample supper. Rows of spotless plates winked from the shelves of the dresser at the far end of the room, and from the rafters overhead hung hams, bundles of dried herbs, nets of onions, and baskets of eggs.

The kindly Badger sat them down on seats to toast themselves at the fire, and made them remove their wet coats and boots. Then he fetched them dressing-gowns and slippers, and bathed the Mole's shin with warm water and mended the cut with sticking-plaster till the whole thing was just as good as new, if not better. In the embracing light and warmth, warm and dry at last, with weary legs propped up in front of them, and the cheering clink of plates being arranged on the table behind, it seemed to the storm-driven animals that the cold and trackless Wild Wood just left outside was miles and miles away, and all that they had suffered in it was a half-forgotten dream.

When at last they were thoroughly toasted, the Badger summoned them to the table, where he had been busy laying a meal. They had felt pretty hungry before, but when they actually saw at last the supper that was spread for them, really it seemed only a question of what they should attack first where all was so attractive, and whether the other things would obligingly wait for them till they had time to give them attention. Conversation was impossible for a long time; and when it was slowly resumed, it was that sort of conversation that comes from talking with your mouth full. The Badger did not mind that sort of thing at all, nor did he take any notice of elbows on the table, or everybody speaking at once. He sat in his armchair at the head of the table, and nodded now and then as the animals told their story; and he did not seem surprised or shocked at anything, and he never said, 'I told you so,' or, 'Just what I always said,' or remarked that they ought to have done so-and-so, or ought not to have

half the room – piles of apples, turnips, and potatoes, baskets full of nuts, and jars of honey; but the two little white beds on the remainder of the floor looked soft and inviting, and the linen on them, though coarse, was clean and smelt beautifully of lavender; and the Mole and the Water Rat, shaking off their clothes in some thirty seconds, tumbled in between the sheets in great joy and contentment.

Following the kindly Badger's advice, the two tired animals came down to breakfast very late next morning, and found a bright fire burning in the kitchen, and two young hedgehogs sitting on a bench at the table, eating oatmeal porridge out of wooden bowls. The hedgehogs dropped their spoons, rose to their feet, and ducked their heads respectfully as the two entered.

'There, sit down, sit down,' said the Rat pleasantly, 'and go on with your porridge. Where have you youngsters come from? Lost your way in the snow, I suppose?'

'Yes, please, sir,' said the elder of the two hedgehogs respectfully. 'Me and little Billy here, we was trying to find our way to school – mother *would* have us go – and of course we lost ourselves, sir, and Billy, he got frightened and took and cried, being young and faint-hearted. And at last we came to Mr Badger's back door, and made so bold as to knock, sir, for Mr Badger, he's a kind-hearted gentleman, as everyone knows.'

'I understand,' said the Rat, cutting himself some rashers from a side of bacon, while the Mole dropped some eggs into a saucepan. 'And what's the weather like outside? You needn't "sir" me quite so much,' he added.

'O, terrible bad, sir, terrible deep the snow is,' said the hedgehog. 'No getting out for the likes of you gentlemen today.'

'Where's Mr Badger?' asked the Mole, as he warmed the coffee-pot before the fire.

'The master's gone into his study, sir,' replied the hedgehog, 'and he said as how he was going to be particular busy this morning, and on no account was he to be disturbed.'

This explanation, of course, was thoroughly understood by everyone present. The animals well knew that Badger, having eaten a hearty breakfast, had retired to his study and settled himself in an armchair with his legs up on another and a red cotton handkerchief over his face, and was being 'busy' in the usual way at this time of the year.

The front door bell clanged loudly, and the Rat, who was very greasy with

buttered toast, sent Billy, the smaller hedgehog, to see who it might be. There was a sound of much stamping in the hall, and presently Billy returned in front of the Otter, who threw himself on the Rat with a hug and a shout of affectionate greeting.

'Get off!' spluttered the Rat, with his mouth full.

'Thought I should find you here all right,' said the Otter cheerfully. 'They were all in a great state of alarm along River Bank when I arrived this morning. Rat never been home all night, nor Mole either, something dreadful must have happened, they said; and the snow had covered up all your tracks, of course. But I knew that when people were in any fix they mostly went to Badger, or else Badger got to know of it somehow, so I came straight off here, through the Wild Wood and the snow! Here, Mole, fry me some slices of ham, like the good little fellow you are. I'm terribly hungry, and I've got any amount to say to Ratty here. Haven't seen him for an age.'

So the good-natured Mole, having cut some slices of ham, set the hedgehogs to fry it, and returned to his own breakfast, while the Otter and the Rat, their heads together, eagerly talked

river-talk, which is endless, running on like the babbling river itself.

A plate of fried ham had just been cleared and sent back for more, when the Badger entered, yawning and rubbing his eyes, and greeted them all in his quiet, simple way, kindly asking after everyone. 'It must be getting on for lunch time,' he remarked to the Otter. 'Better stop and have it with us. You must be hungry, this cold morning.'

'Rather!' replied the Otter, winking at the Mole. 'The sight of these greedy young hedgehogs stuffing themselves with fried ham makes me feel positively famished.'

The hedgehogs, which were just beginning to feel hungry again after their porridge, and after working so hard at their frying, looked timidly up at Mr Badger, but were too shy to say anything.

'Here, you two youngsters be off home to your mother,' said the Badger kindly. 'I'll send someone with you to show you the way. You won't want any dinner today, I'll be bound.'

He gave them sixpence each and a pat on the head, and they went off with much respectful swinging of caps and bowing of heads.

Presently they all sat down to lunch together. The Mole found himself placed next to Mr Badger, and, as the other two were still deep in river-gossip from which nothing could divert them, he took the opportunity to tell Badger how comfortable and home-like it all felt to him. 'Once well underground,' he said, 'you know exactly where you are. Nothing can happen to you, and nothing can get at you. You're entirely your own master, and you don't have to consult anybody or mind what they say. Things go on all the same overhead, and you let 'em, and don't bother about 'em. When you want to, up you go, and there the things are, waiting for you.'

The Badger simply beamed on him. 'That's exactly what I say,' he replied. 'There's no security, or peace, except underground. And then, if your ideas get larger and you want to expand, why, a dig and a scrape, and there you are! If you feel your house is a bit too big, you stop up a hole or two, and there you are again! No builders, no tradesmen, no remarks passed on you by fellows looking over your wall, and, above all, no *weather*. Look at Rat,

now. A couple of feet of flood-water, and he's got to move into hired lodgings; uncomfortable, in a bad position, and horribly expensive. Take Toad. I say nothing against Toad Hall; quite the best house in these parts, *as* a house. But supposing a fire breaks out – where's Toad? Supposing tiles are blown off, or walls sink or crack, or windows get broken – where's Toad? Supposing the rooms are draughty, I *hate* a draught myself – where's Toad? No, up and out of doors is good enough to roam about and get one's living in; but underground to come back to at last: that's my idea of *home*!'

The Mole agreed heartily; and the Badger got very friendly with him. 'When lunch is over,' he said, 'I'll take you all round this little place of mine. I can see you'll appreciate it. You understand what a home ought to be, you do.'

So, after lunch, when the other two had settled themselves into the chimney corner and had started a heated argument on the subject of *eels*, the Badger lighted a lantern and told the Mole to follow him. Crossing the hall, they passed down one of the principal tunnels, and the wavering light of the lantern gave glimpses on either side of rooms both large and small, some mere cupboards, others nearly as broad and imposing as Toad's dining-hall. A narrow passage at right angles led them into another corridor, and here the same thing was repeated. The Mole was staggered at the size and extent of it all; at the length of the dim passages, the solid ceilings of the crammed store chambers, the stonework everywhere, the pillars, the arches, the pavements.

When they got back to the kitchen again, they found the Rat walking up and down, very restless. The underground atmosphere was getting on his nerves, and he seemed really to be afraid that the river would run away if he wasn't there to look after it. So he had his overcoat on, and his pistols thrust into his belt again. 'Come along, Mole,' he said, as soon as he caught sight of them. 'We must get off while it's daylight. Don't want to spend another night in the Wild Wood again.'

'It'll be all right, my fine fellow,' said the Otter. 'I'm coming along with you, and I know every path blindfold; and if there's

a head that needs to be punched, you can rely upon me to punch it.'

'You really needn't fret, Ratty,' added the Badger placidly. 'My passages run further than you think, and I've bolt-holes to the edge of the wood in several directions, though I don't care for everybody to know about them. When you really have to go, you shall leave by one of my short cuts. Meantime, make yourself easy, and sit down again.'

The Rat was nevertheless still eager to be off and attend to his river, so the Badger, taking up his and airless tunnel that wound and dipped for a weary distance that seemed to be miles. At last daylight began to show itself through tangled growth overhanging the mouth of the passage; and the Badger, bidding them a hasty good-bye, pushed them through the opening, made everything look as natural as possible again, with creepers, brushwood, and dead leaves, and retreated.

They found themselves standing on the very edge of the Wild Wood. Rocks and brambles and tree-roots behind them; in front, a great space of quiet fields, hemmed by lines of hedges black on the snow, and, far ahead, a glint of the familiar old river, while the wintry sun hung red and low on the horizon. The Otter, knowing all the paths, took charge of the party, and they trailed out on a beeline for a distant stile. Looking back, they saw the whole mass of the Wild Wood, dense, menacing, compact, grimly set in vast white surroundings; together they turned and made swiftly for home, for firelight, and for the voice, sounding cheerily outside their window, of the river that they knew and trusted in all its moods.

CHAPTER 5

Home Sweet Home

THE sheep ran huddling together against the hurdles, blowing out thin nostrils and stamping with delicate forefeet, their heads thrown back and a light steam rising from the crowded sheep-pen into the frosty air, as the two animals hastened by in high spirits, with much chatter and laughter. They were returning across country after a long day's outing with Otter, hunting and exploring on the wide uplands. The shades of the short winter day were closing in on them, and they had still some distance to go. Plodding across the field, they had heard the sheep and had made for them; and now, leading from the sheep-pen, they found a beaten track that made walking easier.

They plodded along steadily and silently, each of them thinking his own thoughts. The Mole's thoughts ran a good deal on supper, as it was now pitch dark, and it was all a strange country to him as far as he knew, and he was following obediently behind the Rat, leaving the guidance entirely to him. As for the Rat, he was walking a little way ahead, as his habit was, his shoulders humped, his eyes fixed on the straight grey road in front of him; so he did not notice poor Mole when suddenly the call reached him, and took him like an electric shock.

It was one of these mysterious fairy calls from out of the darkness that suddenly reached Mole, making him tingle through and through with its very familiar appeal, even while as yet he could not clearly remember what it was. He stopped dead in his tracks, his nose searching hither and thither in its efforts to recapture the current that had so strongly moved him. A moment, and he had caught it again; and with it this time came recollection in fullest flood.

Home! That was what they meant, those caressing appeals, those soft touches wafted through the air, those invisible little hands pulling and tugging, all one way! Why, it must be quite close by him at that moment, his old home that he had hurriedly forsaken and never sought again, that day when he first found the river! And now it was sending out its scouts and its messengers to capture him and bring him in. Since his escape on that bright morning he had hardly given it a thought, so absorbed had he been in his new life, in all its pleasures, its surprises, its fresh and captivating experiences. Now, with a rush of old memories, how clearly it stood up before him, in the darkness! Shabby indeed, and small and poorly furnished, and yet his, the home he had made for himself, the home he had been so happy to get back to after his day's work. And the home had been happy with him, too, and was missing him, and wanted him back, and was telling him so, through his nose.

The call was clear, the summons was plain. He must obey it instantly, and go. 'Ratty!' he called, full of joyful excitement. 'Hold on! Come back! I want you, quick!'

'O, *come* along, Mole, do!' replied the Rat cheerfully, still plodding along.

'*Please* stop, Ratty!' pleaded the poor Mole. 'You don't understand! It's my home, my old home! I've just come across the smell of it, and it's close by here, really quite close. And I *must* go to it, I must, I must! O, come back, Ratty! Please, please come back!'

The Rat was by this time very far ahead, too far to hear clearly what the Mole was calling, too far to catch the sharp note of painful appeal in his voice. And he was much taken up with the weather, for he too could smell something – something suspiciously like approaching snow.

'Mole, we mustn't stop now, really!' he called back. 'We'll come for it tomorrow, whatever it is you've found. But I daren't stop now: it's late, and the snow's coming on again, and I'm not sure of the way! And I want your nose, Mole, so come on quick, there's a good fellow!' And the Rat pressed forward on his way without waiting for an answer.

Poor Mole stood alone in the road, his heart torn apart, and a big sob gathering, gathering, somewhere

low down inside him. But even under such a test as this his loyalty to his friend stood firm. Never for a moment did he dream of abandoning him. Meanwhile, the wafts from his old home pleaded, whispered, implored, and finally claimed him. He dared not stay any longer within their magic circle. With a wrench that tore his very heart-strings he set his face down the road and followed in the track of the Rat, while faint, thin little smells, still dogging his retreating nose, reproached him for his new friendship and his cruel forgetfulness.

With an effort he caught up the unsuspecting Rat, who began chattering cheerfully about what they would do when they got back, and how fine a fire of logs in the parlour would be, and what a supper he meant to eat; never noticing his friend's silence and troubled state of mind. At last, however, when they had gone some considerable way further, and were passing some tree-stumps at the edge of a copse that bordered the road, he stopped and said kindly, 'Look here, Mole, old chap, you seem dead tired. No talk left in you, and your feet dragging like lead. We'll sit down here for a minute and rest. The snow has held off so far, and the best part of our journey is over.'

The Mole slumped on a tree-stump and tried to control himself, for he felt it surely coming. The sob he had fought with so long refused to be beaten. Up and up, it forced its way to the air, and then another, and another, and others thick and fast; till poor Mole at last gave up the struggle, and cried freely and helplessly and openly, now that he knew it was all over and he had lost what he could hardly be said to have found.

The Rat, astonished and dismayed at the

Mole's grief, did not dare to speak for a while. At last he said, very quietly and sympathetically, 'What is it, old fellow? Whatever can be the matter? Tell us your trouble, and let me see what I can do.'

Poor Mole found it difficult to get any words out between the heavings of his chest that followed one upon another so quickly and held back speech and choked it as it came. 'I know it's a shabby, dingy little place,' he sobbed at last, brokenly: 'not like your cosy quarters or Toad's beautiful hall or Badger's great house, but it was my own little home and I was fond of it, and I went away and forgot all about it, and then I smelt it suddenly on the road, when I called and you wouldn't listen, Rat, and everything came back to me with a rush and I *wanted* it! O dear, O dear, and when you *wouldn't* turn back, Ratty, and I had to leave it, though I was smelling it all the time, I thought my heart would break. We might have just gone and had one look at it, Ratty, only one look. It was close by, but you wouldn't turn back, Ratty, you wouldn't turn back! O dear, O dear!'

The memory brought fresh waves of sorrow, and sobs again took full charge of him, preventing further speech.

The Rat stared straight in front of him, saying nothing, only patting Mole gently on the shoulder. After a time he muttered gloomily, 'I see it all now! What a *pig* I have been! A pig, that's me! Just a pig, a plain pig!'

He waited till Mole's sobs became gradually less, till at last sniffs were frequent and sobs came only now and then. Then he rose from his seat, and, remarking carelessly, 'Well, now we'd really better be getting on, old chap!' set off up the road again, over the difficult way they had come.

'Wherever are you (hic) going to (hic), Ratty?' cried the tearful Mole, looking up in alarm.

'We're going to find that home of yours, old fellow,' replied the Rat pleasantly, 'so you had better come along, for it will take some finding, and we shall want your nose.'

'O, come back, Ratty, do!' cried the Mole, getting up and hurrying after him. 'It's no good, I tell you! It's too late, and too dark, and the place is too far off, and the snow's coming! And – and I never meant to let you know

I was feeling that way about it – it was all an accident and a mistake! And think of River Bank, and your supper!'

'Hang River Bank, and supper too!' said the Rat heartily. 'I tell you, I'm going to find this place now, if I stay out all night. So cheer up, old chap, and take my arm, and we'll very soon be back there again.'

Still snuffling, pleading, and reluctant, Mole let himself be dragged back along the road by his companion. When at last it seemed to the Rat that they must be nearing that part of the road where the Mole had been held up, he said, 'Now, no more talking. Business! Use your nose, and give your mind to it.'

They moved on in silence for some little way, when suddenly the Rat was conscious, through his arm that was linked in Mole's, of a faint sort of electric thrill that was passing down that animal's body. Instantly he disengaged himself, fell back a pace, and waited, all attention.

The signals were coming through!

Mole stood a moment rigid, while his uplifted nose, quivering slightly, felt the air.

The Rat, much excited, kept close to his heels as the Mole, with something of the air of a sleep-walker, crossed a dry ditch, scrambled through a hedge, and nosed his way over a field open and trackless and bare in the faint starlight.

Suddenly, without giving warning, he dived; but the Rat was on the alert, and promptly followed him down the tunnel to which the Mole's nose had faithfully led him.

It was close and airless, and the earthy smell was strong, and it seemed a long time to Rat before the passage ended and he could stand up and stretch and shake himself. The Mole struck a match, and by its light the Rat saw that they were standing in an open space, neatly swept and sanded underfoot, and directly facing them was Mole's little front door, with 'Mole End' painted, in Gothic lettering, over the bell-pull at the side.

Mole reached down a lantern from a nail on the wall and lit it, and the Rat, looking round him, saw that they were in a sort of forecourt. A garden seat stood on one side of the door, and on the other, a roller; for the Mole, who was a tidy animal when at home, could not stand having his ground kicked up by other animals into little runs that ended in earth-heaps. On the walls hung wire baskets with ferns in them, alternating with brackets carrying plaster statues. Down one side of the forecourt ran a skittle alley, with benches along it and little wooden tables marked with rings that hinted at beer mugs. In the middle was a small round pond containing goldfish and surrounded by a cockleshell border. Out of the centre of the pond rose a fanciful ornament clothed in more cockleshells and topped by a large silvered glass ball that reflected everything all wrong and had a very pleasing effect.

Mole's face beamed at the sight of all these objects so dear to him, and he hurried Rat through the door, lit a lamp in the hall, and took one glance round his old home. He saw the dust lying thick on everything, saw the cheerless, deserted look of the long-neglected house, and its modest size, its worn and shabby contents, and collapsed again on a hall chair, his nose in his paws. 'O, Ratty!' he cried dismally, 'why ever did I do it? Why did I bring you to this poor, cold little place, on a night like this, when you might have been at River Bank by this time, toasting your toes before a blazing fire, with all your own nice things about you!'

The Rat paid no attention. He was running here and there, opening doors, inspecting rooms and cupboards, and lighting lamps and candles and sticking them up everywhere. 'What a capital little house this is!' he called out cheerily. 'So compact! So well planned! Everything here and everything in its place! We'll make a fine night of it. The first thing we want is a good fire; I'll see to that – I always know where to find things. So this is the parlour? Splendid! Your own idea, those little sleeping-bunks in the wall? Capital! Now, I'll fetch the wood and the coals, and you get a duster, Mole, you'll find one in the drawer of the kitchen table, and try and smarten things up a bit. Bustle about, old chap!'

Encouraged by his companion, the Mole roused himself and dusted and polished with energy and heartiness, while the Rat, running to and fro with armfuls of fuel, soon had a cheerful blaze roaring up the chimney. He called the Mole to come and warm himself; but Mole promptly had another fit of the blues, dropping down on a couch in dark despair and burying his face in his duster.

'Rat,' he moaned, 'how about your supper, you poor, cold, hungry,

weary animal? I've nothing to give you, nothing, not a crumb!'

'What a fellow you are for giving in!' said the Rat reproachfully. 'Why, only just now I saw a sardine opener on the kitchen dresser, quite distinctly; and everybody knows that means there are sardines about somewhere. Come on! Pull yourself together, and let's look around.'

So, they went hunting through every cupboard and turned out every drawer. The result was not so very depressing after all, though of course it might have been better; a tin of sardines, a box of captain's biscuits, nearly full, and a German sausage encased in silver paper.

'There's a banquet for you!' observed the Rat, as he arranged the table. 'I know some animals who would give their ears to be sitting down to supper with us tonight!'

'No bread!' groaned the Mole. 'No butter, no –'

'No *pâté de foie gras*, no champagne!' continued the Rat, grinning. 'And that reminds me: what's that little door at the end of the passage? Your cellar, of course! Every luxury in this house! Just you wait a minute.'

He made for the cellar door, and presently reappeared, somewhat dusty, with a bottle of beer in each paw and another under each arm. 'Self-indulgent beggar you seem to be, Mole,' he observed. 'Deny yourself nothing. This is really the nicest little place I was ever in. Now, wherever did you pick up those prints? Make the place look so home-like, they do. No wonder you're so fond of it, Mole. Tell me all about it, and how you came to make it what it is.'

Then, while the Rat busied himself fetching plates, and knives and forks, and mustard which he mixed in an egg-cup, the Mole related – somewhat shyly at first, but with more freedom as he warmed to his subject – how this was planned, and how that was thought out, and how this was got through a windfall from an aunt, and that was a wonderful find and a bargain, and this other thing was bought with hard-earned savings and a certain amount of 'going without'. His spirits finally quite restored, he had to go and touch his possessions, and take a lamp and show off their points to his visitor, and tell him all about them, quite forgetful of the supper they both so much needed. Rat, who was desperately hungry but tried to conceal it, nodded seriously, examining with a puckered brow, and saying, 'Wonderful', and 'Most remarkable', at intervals, when the chance for an observation was given him.

At last the Rat succeeded in luring him to the table, and had just got seriously to work with the sardine opener when sounds were heard from the forecourt outside: sounds like the scuffling of small feet in the gravel and a confused murmur of tiny voices, while broken sentences reached them. 'Now, all in a line – hold the lantern up a bit, Tommy – clear your throats first – no coughing after I say one, two, three. Where's young Bill? Here, come on, do, we're all a-waiting –'

'What's up?' asked the Rat.

'I think it must be the fieldmice,' replied the Mole, with a touch of pride in his manner. 'They go round carol singing regularly at this time of the year. And they never pass me over: they come to Mole End last of all; and I used to give them hot drinks, and supper too sometimes, when I could afford it. It will be like old times to hear them again.'

'Let's have a look at them!' cried the Rat, jumping up and running to the door.

It was a pretty sight that met their eyes when they flung the door open. In the forecourt, lit by the dim rays of a horn lantern, some eight or ten little fieldmice stood in a semicircle, red woolly scarves round their necks, their forepaws thrust deep into their pockets, their feet jigging for warmth. With bright beady eyes they glanced shyly at each other, sniggering a little, sniffing and using their coat sleeves a good deal. As the door opened, one of the elder ones that carried the lantern was just saying, 'Now then, one, two, three!' and right away their shrill little voices arose, singing one of the old-time carols that their forefathers had composed and handed down to be sung at Yule-time.

CAROL
Villagers all, this frosty tide,
Let your doors swing open wide,
Though wind may follow, and snow beside,
Yet draw us in by your fire to bide;
Joy shall be yours in the morning!

Here we stand in the cold and the sleet,
Blowing fingers and stamping feet,
Come from far away you to greet –
You by the fire and we in the street –
Bidding you joy in the morning!

For ere one half of the night was gone,
Sudden a star has led us on,
Raining bliss and benison,
Bliss tomorrow and more anon,
Joy for every morning!

Goodman Joseph toiled through the snow,
Saw the star o'er a stable low;
Mary she might not further go –
Welcome thatch, and litter below!
Joy was hers in the morning!

And then they heard the angels tell
'Who were the first to cry Noël?
Animals all, as it befell,
In the stable where they did dwell!
Joy shall be theirs in the morning!'

The voices stopped, the singers, shy but smiling, looked at each other, and silence fell, but for a moment only. Then, from up above and far away, came the sound of distant bells ringing a loud and joyful peal.

'Very well sung, boys!' cried the Rat heartily. 'And now come along in, all of you, and warm yourselves by the fire, and have something hot!'

'Yes, come along, fieldmice,' cried the Mole eagerly. 'This is quite like old times! Shut the door after you. Pull up that seat to the fire. Now, you just wait a minute, while we – O, Ratty!' he cried in despair, plumping down on a seat, close to tears. 'Whatever are we doing? We've nothing to give them!'

'You leave all that to me,' said the masterful Rat. 'Here, you with the lantern! Come over this way. I want to talk to you. Now, tell me, are there any shops open at this hour of the night?'

'Why, certainly, sir,' replied the fieldmouse respectfully. 'At this time of the year our shops keep open to all sorts of hours.'

'Then look here!' said the Rat. 'You go off at once, you and your lantern, and you get me...'

Here much muttered conversation took place, and the Mole only heard bits of it. Finally, there was a chink of coin passing from paw to paw, the fieldmouse was provided with an ample basket for his purchases, and off he hurried, he and his lantern.

The rest of the fieldmice, perched in a row on the seat, their small legs swinging, gave themselves up to enjoyment of the fire, and toasted their toes till they tingled; while the Mole, failing to draw them into easy conversation, plunged into family history and made each of them recite the names of his numerous brothers, who were too young, it appeared, to be allowed to go out carolling this year.

The Rat, meanwhile, was busy examining the label on one of the beer bottles. 'I perceive this to be Old Burton,' he remarked approvingly. '*Sensible* Mole! The very thing! Now we shall be able to mull some ale! Get the things ready, Mole, while I draw the corks.'

It did not take long to prepare the brew and thrust the tin heater well into the red heart of the fire; and soon every fieldmouse was sipping and coughing and choking (for a little mulled ale goes a long way) and wiping his eyes and laughing and forgetting he had ever been cold in all his life.

Then the latch clicked, the door opened, and the fieldmouse with the lantern reappeared, staggering under the weight of his basket. Under the generalship of Rat, everybody was set to do something or to fetch something. In a very few minutes supper was ready, and Mole, as he took the head of the table in a sort of dream, saw the board set thick with tasty treats; saw his little friends' faces brighten and beam as they fell to without delay; and then let himself loose on the food so magically provided, thinking what a happy home-coming this had turned out, after all. As they ate, they talked of old times, and the fieldmice gave him the local gossip up to date, and answered as well as they could the hundred questions he had to ask them. The Rat said little or nothing, only taking care that each guest had what he wanted, and plenty of it, and that Mole had no

trouble or worry about anything.

They clattered off at last, very grateful and showering wishes of the season, with their jacket pockets stuffed with presents for the small brothers and sisters at home. When the door had closed on the last of them and the chink of the lanterns had died away, Mole and Rat kicked the fire up, drew their chairs in, brewed themselves a last nightcap of mulled ale, and discussed the events of the long day. At last the Rat, with a tremendous yawn, said, 'Mole, old chap, I'm ready to drop. Sleepy is simply not the word. That your own bunk over on that side? Very well, then, I'll take this. What a grand little house this is! Everything so handy!'

He clambered into his bunk and rolled himself well up in the blankets, and sleep soon carried him away.

The weary Mole also was glad to turn in without delay, and soon had his head on his pillow, in great joy and contentment. But before he closed his eyes he let them wander round his old room, mellow in the glow of the firelight that played or rested on all the familiar and friendly things. He was now in just the frame of mind that the tactful Rat had quietly worked to bring about in him. He saw clearly how plain and simple, how narrow, even, it all was; but clearly, too, how much it all meant to him. He did not at all want to abandon the new life and its splendid spaces, to turn his back on sun and air and all they offered him, and creep home and stay there; the upper world was all too strong, it called to him still, even down there, and he knew he must return to it. But it was good to think he had this to come back to, this place which was all his own, these things which were so glad to see him again and could always be counted upon for the same simple welcome.

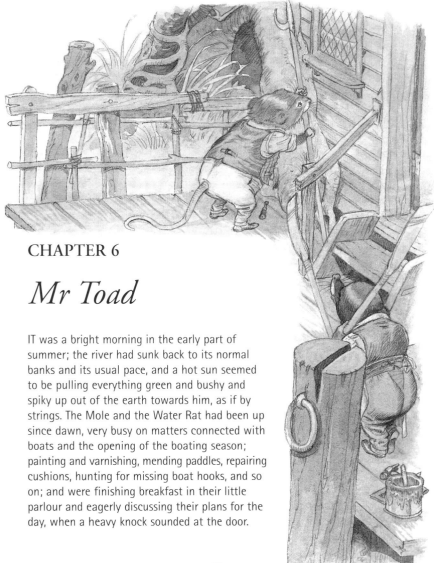

CHAPTER 6

Mr Toad

IT was a bright morning in the early part of summer; the river had sunk back to its normal banks and its usual pace, and a hot sun seemed to be pulling everything green and bushy and spiky up out of the earth towards him, as if by strings. The Mole and the Water Rat had been up since dawn, very busy on matters connected with boats and the opening of the boating season; painting and varnishing, mending paddles, repairing cushions, hunting for missing boat hooks, and so on; and were finishing breakfast in their little parlour and eagerly discussing their plans for the day, when a heavy knock sounded at the door.

'Bother!' said the Rat, egg all over him. 'See who it is, Mole, like a good fellow, since you've finished.'

The Mole went to answer the door, and the Rat heard him utter a cry of surprise. Then he flung the parlour door open, and announced with much importance, 'Mr Badger!'

This was a wonderful thing, indeed, that the Badger should pay a call on them, or indeed on anybody. He generally had to be caught, if you wanted him badly, as he slipped quietly along a hedgerow in the early morning or late evening, or else be hunted up in his own house in the middle of the wood.

The Badger strode heavily into the room, and stood looking at the two animals with an expression full of seriousness. The Rat let his egg-spoon fall on the tablecloth, and sat open-mouthed.

'The hour has come!' said the Badger at last.

'What hour?' asked the Rat uneasily, glancing at the clock on the mantelpiece.

'*Whose* hour, you should rather say,' replied the Badger. 'Why, Toad's hour! The hour of Toad! I said I would take him in hand as soon as the winter was well over, and I'm going to take him in hand today!'

'Toad's hour, of course!' cried the Mole delightedly. 'Hooray! I remember now! *We'll* teach him to be a sensible Toad!'

'This very morning,' continued the Badger, taking an armchair, 'as I learnt last night from a trustworthy source, another new and very powerful motor-car will arrive at Toad Hall on approval or return. At this very moment, perhaps, Toad is busily putting on those quite hideous clothes so dear to him, which transform him from a (fairly) good-looking Toad into an Object which throws any decent-minded animal that comes across it into a violent fit. We must be up and doing, before it is too late. You two animals will accompany me instantly to Toad Hall, and the work of rescue shall be accomplished.'

'Right you are!' cried the Rat, starting up. 'We'll rescue the poor unhappy animal! We'll change him! He'll be the most changed Toad that ever was before we've done with him!'

They set off up the road, Badger leading the way. They reached the carriage drive of Toad Hall to find, as the Badger had expected, a shiny new motor-car, of great size, painted a bright red, standing in front of the house. As they neared the door it was flung open, and Mr Toad, dressed in goggles, cap, gaiters, and enormous overcoat, came swaggering down the steps, drawing on his gloves.

'Hullo! Come on, you fellows!' he cried cheerfully on catching sight of them. 'You're just in time to come with me for a – to come for a – for a – er –'

His hearty voice fell away as he noticed the stern unbending look on the faces of his silent friends, and his invitation remained unfinished.

The Badger strode up the steps. 'Take him inside,' he said sternly to his companions. Then, as Toad was hustled through the door, struggling and protesting, he turned to the chauffeur in charge of the new motor-car.

'I'm afraid you won't be wanted today,' he said. 'Mr Toad has changed his mind. He will not require the car. Please understand that this is final. You needn't wait.' Then he followed the others inside and shut the door.

'Now, then!' he said to the Toad, when the four of them stood together in the hall. 'First of all, take those ridiculous things off!'

'Shan't!' replied Toad, with great spirit. 'What is the meaning of this outrage?

I demand an instant explanation.'

'Take them off him, then, you two,' ordered the Badger briefly.

They had to lay Toad out on the floor, kicking and calling all sorts of names, before they could get to work properly. Then the Rat sat on him, and the Mole got his motor clothes off him bit by bit, and they stood him up on his legs again. A good deal of his fiery spirit seemed to have disappeared with the removal of his fine clothes. Now that he was merely Toad, and no longer the Terror of the Highway, he giggled feebly and looked from one to the other appealingly.

'You knew it must come to this, sooner or later, Toad,' the Badger explained severely. 'You've disregarded all the warnings we've given you, you've gone on wasting the money your father left you, and you're getting us animals a bad name in the district by your furious driving and your smashes and your rows with the police. Independence is all very well, but we animals never allow our friends to make fools of themselves beyond a certain limit; and that limit you've reached. Now, you're a good fellow in many respects, and I don't want to be too hard on you. I'll make one more effort to bring you to reason. You will come with me into the smoking room, and there you will hear some facts about yourself; and we'll see whether you come out of that room the same Toad that you went in.'

He took Toad firmly by the arm, led him into the smoking room, and closed the door behind them.

'*That's* no good!' said the Rat. '*Talking* to Toad'll never cure him. He'll *say* anything.'

They made themselves comfortable in armchairs and waited patiently. Through the closed door they could just hear the long drone of the Badger's voice, rising and falling in waves; and presently they heard long-drawn sobs,

seeming to come from Toad, who was a soft-hearted and affectionate fellow, very easily converted for the time being to any point of view.

After some three-quarters of an hour the door opened, and the Badger reappeared, leading by the paw a very limp and dejected Toad. His skin hung baggily about him, his legs wobbled, and his cheeks were lined with tears.

'Sit down there, Toad,' said the Badger kindly, pointing to a chair. 'My friends,' he went on, 'I am pleased to inform you that Toad has at last seen the error of his ways. He is truly sorry for his misguided conduct in the past, and he has agreed to give up motor-cars entirely and for ever. I have his solemn promise to that effect.'

'That is very good news,' said the Mole gravely.

'Very good news indeed,' said the Rat doubtfully, 'if only, *if* only –'

He was looking very hard at Toad as he said this, and could not help thinking he saw something like a twinkle in that animal's still sorrowful eyes.

'There's only one thing more to be done,' continued the Badger. 'Toad, I want you to repeat, before your friends here, what you fully admitted to me in the smoking-room just now. First, you are sorry for what you've done, and you see the folly of it all?'

There was a long, long pause. Toad looked this way and that, while the other animals waited in silence. At last he spoke.

'No!' he said a little sulkily, but stoutly. 'I'm *not* sorry. And it wasn't folly at all! It was simply glorious!'

'What?' cried the Badger, greatly shocked. 'You backsliding animal, didn't you tell me just now, in there –',

'O, yes, yes, in *there*,' said Toad impatiently. 'I'd have said anything in there. You're so eloquent, dear Badger, and so moving, and so convincing, and put all your points so very well. You can do what you like with me in *there*, and you know it. But I've been searching my mind since, and going over things in it, and I find that I'm not a bit sorry really, so it's no earthly good saying I am; now, is it?'

'Then you don't promise,' said the Badger, 'never to touch a motor-car again?'

'Certainly not!' replied Toad. 'On the contrary, I faithfully promise that the very first motor-car I see, *poop-poop*! off I go in it!'

'Told you so, didn't I?' said the Rat to the Mole.

'Very well, then,' said the Badger firmly, rising to his feet. 'Since you won't be reasonable, we'll try what force can do. I feared it would come to this all along. You've often asked us three to come and stay with you, Toad, in this handsome house of yours; well, now we're going to. When we've converted you to a proper point of view we may quit, but not before. Take him upstairs, you two, and lock him up in his bedroom, while we arrange matters between ourselves.'

'It's for your own good, Toady, you know,' said the Rat kindly, as Toad, kicking and struggling, was hauled up the stairs by his two faithful friends. 'Think what fun we shall all have together, just as we used to, when you've quite got over this painful attack of yours!'

'We'll take great care of everything for you till you're well, Toad,' said the Mole, 'and we'll see your money isn't wasted, as it has been.'

'No more of those regrettable incidents with the police, Toad,' said the Rat, as they thrust him into his bedroom.

'And no more weeks in hospital, being ordered about by female nurses, Toad,' added the Mole, turning the key on him.

They went downstairs, Toad shouting abuse at them through the keyhole; and the three friends then met in conference on the situation.

'It's going to be a tiresome business,' said the Badger, sighing. 'I've never seen Toad so determined. However, we will see it out. He must never be left an instant unguarded. We shall have to take it in turns to be with him, till the poison has worked itself out of his system.'

They arranged to keep watch over him. Each animal took it in turns to sleep in Toad's room at night, and they divided the day up between them.

At first Toad was very trying to his careful guardians. When his violent fits took him he would arrange bedroom chairs to look like a motor-car and would crouch on the front one bent forward and staring ahead, making horrible noises, till the climax was reached, when, turning a complete somersault, he would lie face down among the ruins of the chairs, apparently completely satisfied for the moment. As time passed, however, these painful attacks grew less frequent, and his friends tried hard to make him think of new things. But his interest in other matters did not seem to revive, and he grew weak and depressed.

One fine morning the Rat, whose turn it was to go on duty, went upstairs to relieve Badger, whom he found fidgeting to be off and stretch his legs in a long ramble round his wood and down his earths and burrows. 'Toad's still in bed,' he told the Rat, outside the door. 'Can't get much out of him, except, "O, leave me alone, I want nothing, perhaps I'll be better presently, it may pass off in time, don't be unduly anxious," and so on. Now, you look out, Rat! When Toad's quiet and obedient, then he's at his most artful. There's sure to be something up. I know him. Well, now I must be off.'

'How are you today, old chap?' asked

the Rat cheerfully, as he approached Toad's bedside.

He had to wait some minutes for an answer. At last a feeble voice replied, 'Thank you so much, dear Ratty! So good of you to ask! But first tell me how you are yourself, and the excellent Mole?'

'O, *we're* all right,' replied the Rat. 'Mole,' he added carelessly, 'is going out for a run round with Badger. They'll be out till lunch-time, so you and I will spend a pleasant morning together, and I'll do my best to amuse you. Now jump up, there's a good fellow, and don't lie moping there on a fine morning like this!'

'Dear, kind Rat,' murmured Toad, 'how little you realise my condition, and how very far I am from "jumping up" now if ever! But do not trouble about me. I hate being a burden to my friends, and I do not expect to be one much longer. Indeed, I almost hope not.'

'Well, I hope not, too,' said the Rat heartily. 'You've been a fine bother to us all this time, and I'm glad to hear it's going to stop. And in weather like this, and the boating season just beginning! It's too bad of you, Toad! It isn't the trouble we mind, but you're making us miss such an awful lot.'

'I'm afraid it *is* the trouble you mind, though,' replied the Toad feebly. 'I can quite understand it. It's natural enough. You're tired of bothering about me. I mustn't ask you to do anything further. I'm a nuisance, I know.'

'You are, indeed,' said the Rat. 'But I tell you, I'd take any trouble on earth for you, if only you'd be a sensible animal.'

'If I thought that, Ratty,' murmured Toad, more feebly than ever, 'then I would beg you – for the last time, probably – to step round to the village as quickly as possible – even now it may be too late – and fetch the doctor. But don't you bother. It's only a trouble, and perhaps we may as well let things take their course.'

'Why, what do you want a doctor for?' asked the Rat, coming closer and examining him. He certainly lay very still and flat, and his voice was weaker and his manner much changed.

'Surely you have noticed of late,' murmured Toad. 'But no, why should you? Noticing things is only a trouble. Tomorrow, indeed, you may be saying

to yourself, "O, if only I had noticed sooner! If only I had done something!" But no; it's a trouble. Never mind, forget that I asked.'

'Look here, old man,' said the Rat, beginning to get rather alarmed, 'of course I'll fetch a doctor to you, if you really think you want him. But you can hardly be bad enough for that yet. Let's talk about something else.'

'I fear, dear friend,' said Toad, with a sad smile, 'that "talk" can do little in a case like this, or doctors either, for that matter; still, one must grasp at the slightest straw. And, by the way, while you are about it, I *hate* to give you more trouble, but I happen to remember that you will pass the door, would you mind at the same time asking the lawyer to step up? It would be a convenience to me, and there are moments, perhaps I should say there is a moment, when one must face disagreeable tasks, at whatever cost to exhausted nature!'

A lawyer! O, he must be really bad! the worried Rat said to himself, as he hurried from the room, not forgetting, however, to lock the door carefully behind him.

Outside, he stopped to consider. The other two were far away, and he had no one to consult.

'It's best to be on the safe side,' he said. 'I've known Toad fancy himself frightfully bad before, without the slightest reason; but I've never heard him ask for a lawyer! If there's nothing really the matter, the doctor will tell him he's an old fool, and cheer him up; it won't take very long.' So he ran off to the village on his errand of mercy.

The Toad, who had hopped lightly out of bed as soon as he heard the key turned in the lock, watched him eagerly from the window till he disappeared down the drive. Then, laughing heartily, he dressed as quickly as possible in the smartest suit he could lay hands on at the moment, filled his pockets with cash which he took from a small drawer in the dressing-table, and next, knotting the sheets from his bed together and tying one end round the central bar of the window, he scrambled out, slid lightly to the ground, and, taking the opposite direction to the Rat, marched off lightheartedly, whistling a merry tune.

It was a gloomy lunch for Rat when the Badger and the Mole at length returned, and he had to face them at table with his rather weak story. The Badger's biting, not to say brutal, remarks may be imagined; but it was painful to the Rat that even the Mole, though he took his friend's side as far as possible, could not help saying,
'You've been a bit of a duffer this time, Ratty! Toad, too, of all animals!'

'He did it awfully well,' said the Rat.

'He did *you* awfully well!' replied the Badger hotly. 'However, talking won't mend matters. He's got clear away for the time, that's certain; and the worst of it is, he'll be so conceited with what he'll think is his cleverness that he may do anything. One comfort is, we're free now, and needn't waste any more of our precious time doing sentry duty. But we'd better continue to sleep at Toad Hall for a while longer. Toad may be brought back at any moment on a stretcher, or between two policemen.'

So spoke the Badger, not knowing what the future held in store, or how much water was to run under bridges before Toad should sit at ease again in his ancestral Hall.

Meanwhile, Toad was walking briskly along the high road, some miles from home. At first he had taken by-paths, and crossed many fields, and changed his course several times, in case of pursuit; but now, feeling by this time safe from recapture, and the sun smiling brightly on him, he almost danced along the road.

'Smart piece of work that!' he remarked to himself, chuckling. 'Brain against brute force, and brain came out on the top as it's bound to do. Poor old Ratty! My! Won't he catch it when the Badger gets back! A worthy fellow, Ratty, with many good qualities, but very little intelligence and absolutely no education. I must take him in hand some day, and see if I can make something of him.'

Filled full of conceited thoughts such as these he strode along, his head in the air, till he reached a little town, where the sign of The Red Lion, swinging across the road halfway down the main street, reminded him that he had not had breakfast that day, and that he was very hungry after his long walk. He marched into the inn, ordered the best lunch that could be provided at so short a notice, and sat down to eat it in the coffee room.

He was about halfway through his meal

when an only too familiar sound, approaching down the street, made him start and fall trembling all over. The *poop-poop!* drew nearer and nearer, the car could be heard to turn into the inn yard and come to a stop, and Toad had to hold on to the leg of the table to hide his feelings. Presently the party entered the coffee room, hungry and talkative. Toad listened eagerly, all ears, for a time; at last he could stand it no longer. He slipped out of the room quietly, paid his bill at the bar, and as soon as he got outside, sauntered round quietly to the inn yard. 'There cannot be any harm,' he said to himself, 'in my only just *looking* at it!'

The car stood in the middle of the yard, quite unattended, the stable helps being all at their dinner. Toad walked slowly round it, inspecting, criticising, thinking deeply.

'I wonder,' he said to himself presently, 'I wonder if this sort of car *starts* easily?'

Next moment, hardly knowing how it came about, he found he had hold of the handle and was turning it. As the familiar sound broke forth, the old passion came back and completely mastered Toad, body and soul. As if in a dream he found himself, somehow, seated in the driver's seat; as if in a dream, he pulled the lever and swung the car round the yard and out through the archway; and, as if in a dream, all sense of right and wrong seemed temporarily suspended. He increased his pace, and as the car leapt forth on the high road through the open country, he only knew that he was Toad once more, Toad at his best and highest, Toad the Terror, the Lord of the Lone Trail, before whom all must give

way. The miles were eaten up under him as he sped he knew not where, living his hour, not caring what might happen to him.

* * * * * * * * * * * *

'To my mind,' observed the Chairman of the Bench of Magistrates cheerfully, 'the *only* difficulty that presents itself in this otherwise very clear case is, how we can possibly make it sufficiently hot for the incorrigible rogue and hardened ruffian whom we see cowering in the dock before us. Let me see: he has been found guilty, on the clearest evidence, first, of stealing a valuable motor-car; secondly, of driving to the public danger; and, thirdly, of gross impertinence to the police. Mr Clerk, will you tell us, please, what is the very stiffest penalty we can impose for each of these offences? Without, of course, giving the prisoner the benefit of any doubt, because there isn't any.'

The Clerk scratched his nose with his pen. 'Some people would consider,' he observed, 'that stealing the motor-car was the worst offence; and so it is. But cheeking the police undoubtedly carries the severest penalty; and so it ought. Supposing you were to say twelve months for the theft, which is mild; and three years for the furious driving, which is lenient; and fifteen years for the cheek, which was pretty bad sort of cheek, judging by what we've heard from the witness box, those figures, if added together correctly, tot up to nineteen years –'

'First rate!' said the Chairman.

'– So you had better make it a round twenty years and be on the safe side,' ended the Clerk.

'An excellent suggestion!' said the Chairman approvingly. 'Prisoner! Pull yourself together and try and stand up straight. It's going to be twenty years for you this time. And mind, if you appear before us again, upon any charge whatever, we shall have to deal with you very seriously!'

Then the brutal minions of the law fell upon the hapless Toad; loaded him with chains, and dragged him from the Court House, shrieking, praying, protesting; till they reached the door of the grimmest dungeon that lay in the heart of the innermost keep. There they paused, where an ancient jailer sat fingering a bunch of mighty keys.

'Oddsbodikins!' said the Sergeant of Police, taking off his helmet and wiping his forehead. 'Get up, old loon, and take over from us this vile Toad, a criminal of deepest guilt and matchless artfulness and resource. Watch and guard him with all your skill; and mark well, greybeard, should anything untoward befall, your old head shall answer for his!'

The jailer nodded grimly, laying his withered hand on the shoulder of the miserable Toad. The rusty key creaked in the lock, the great door clanged behind them; and Toad was a helpless prisoner in the remotest dungeon of the best guarded keep of the stoutest castle in all the length and breadth of Merry England.

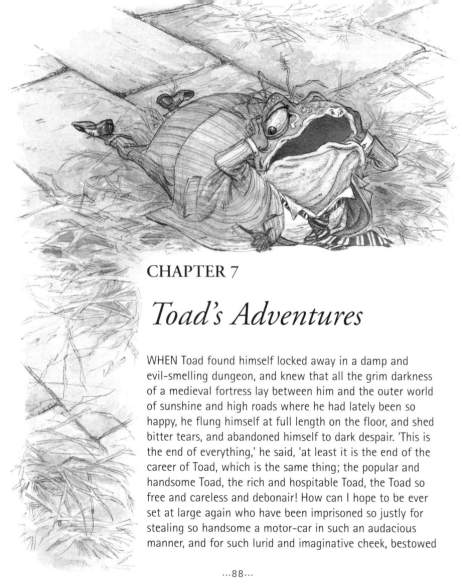

CHAPTER 7

Toad's Adventures

WHEN Toad found himself locked away in a damp and evil-smelling dungeon, and knew that all the grim darkness of a medieval fortress lay between him and the outer world of sunshine and high roads where he had lately been so happy, he flung himself at full length on the floor, and shed bitter tears, and abandoned himself to dark despair. 'This is the end of everything,' he said, 'at least it is the end of the career of Toad, which is the same thing; the popular and handsome Toad, the rich and hospitable Toad, the Toad so free and careless and debonair! How can I hope to be ever set at large again who have been imprisoned so justly for stealing so handsome a motor-car in such an audacious manner, and for such lurid and imaginative cheek, bestowed upon such a number of fat, red-faced policemen!' Here his sobs choked him. 'Stupid animal that I was, now I must languish in this dungeon, till people who were proud to say they knew me, have forgotten the very name of Toad! O wise old Badger! 'O clever, intelligent Rat and sensible Mole! What sound judgments, what a knowledge of men and matters you possess! O unhappy and forsaken Toad!' With lamentations such as these he passed his days and nights for several weeks, refusing his meals or light refreshments, though the grim and ancient jailer, knowing that Toad's pockets were well lined, frequently pointed out that many comforts, and indeed luxuries, could by arrangement be sent in – at a price – from outside.

Now the jailer had a pleasant and good-hearted daughter, who assisted her father in the lighter duties of his post. She was particularly fond of animals, and, besides her canary, she kept several piebald mice and a restless squirrel. This kind-hearted girl, pitying the misery of Toad, said to her father one day, 'Father! I can't bear to see that poor beast so unhappy, and getting so thin! You let me have the managing of him. You know how fond of animals I am. I'll make him eat from my hand, and sit up, and do all sorts of things.'

Her father replied that she could do what she liked with him. He was tired of Toad, and his sulks and his airs and his meanness. So that day she went on her errand of mercy, and knocked at the door of Toad's cell.

'Now, cheer up, Toad,' she said coaxingly, on entering, 'and sit up and dry your eyes and be a sensible animal. And do try and eat a bit of dinner. See, I've brought you some of mine, hot from the oven!'

It was bubble-and-squeak, between two plates, and its fragrance filled the narrow cell. The penetrating smell of cabbage reached the

nose of Toad as he lay in his misery on the floor. It gave him the idea for a moment that perhaps life was not such a blank and desperate thing as he had imagined. But still he wailed, and kicked with his legs, and refused to be comforted. So the wise girl retired for the time, but, of course, a good deal of the smell of hot cabbage remained behind, as it will do, and Toad, between his sobs, sniffed and reflected, and gradually began to think new and inspiring thoughts: of chivalry, and poetry, and deeds still to be done. The air of the narrow cell took on a rosy tinge; he began to think of his friends, and how they would surely be able to do something; of lawyers, and how they would have enjoyed his case, and what a fool he had been not to get in a few; and lastly, he thought of his own great cleverness, and all that he was capable of if he only gave his great mind to it; and the cure was almost complete.

When the girl returned, some hours later, she carried a tray, with a cup of fragrant tea steaming on it; and a plate piled up with very hot buttered toast, cut thick, very brown on both sides, with the butter running through the holes in it in great golden drops, like honey from the honeycomb. The smell of that buttered toast simply talked to Toad, and with no uncertain voice; talked of warm kitchens, of breakfasts on bright frosty mornings, and of snug parlour firesides on winter evenings. Toad sat up on end once more, dried his eyes, sipped his tea and munched his toast, and soon began talking freely about himself, and the house he lived in, and his doings there, and how important he was, and what a lot his friends thought of him.

The jailer's daughter saw that the topic was doing him as much good as the tea, as indeed it was, and encouraged him to go on.

'Tell me about Toad Hall,' said she. 'It sounds beautiful.'

'Toad Hall,' said the Toad proudly, 'is a self-contained gentleman's residence, very unique; dating in part from the fourteenth century, but with every modern convenience. Up-to-date sanitation. Five minutes from church, post office, and golf links. Suitable for –'.

'Bless the animal,' said the girl, laughing, 'I don't want to *take* it. Tell me something *real* about it. But first wait till I fetch you some more tea and toast.'

She tripped away, and presently returned with a fresh trayful; and Toad, pitching into the toast eagerly, his spirits quite restored to their usual level, told her about the boat house, and the fish pond, and the old walled kitchen garden; and about the pig sties, and the stables, and the pigeon house, and the hen house; and about the dairy, and the wash house, and the china cupboards, and the linen presses (she liked that bit especially); and about the banqueting hall, and the fun they had there when the other animals were gathered round the table and Toad was at his best, singing songs, telling stories, carrying on generally.

Then she wanted to know about his animal friends, and was very interested in all he had to tell her about them and how they lived, and what they did to pass their time. Of course, she did not say she was fond of animals as *pets*, because she had the sense to see that Toad would be extremely offended. When she said good night, having filled his water jug and shaken up his straw for him, Toad was very much the same self-satisfied animal that he had been of old. He sang a little song or two, of the sort he used to sing at his dinner parties, curled

himself up in the straw, and had an excellent night's rest and the pleasantest of dreams.

They had many interesting talks together, after that, as the dreary days went on; and the jailer's daughter grew very sorry for Toad, and thought it a great shame that a poor little animal should be locked up in prison for what seemed to her a very unimportant crime. Toad, of course, in his vanity, thought that her interest in him came from a growing tenderness; and he could not help half regretting that the social gulf between them was so very wide, for she was a pretty lass, and evidently admired him.

One morning the girl was very thoughtful and did not seem to Toad to be paying proper attention to his witty sayings and sparkling comments.

'Toad,' she said presently, 'just listen, please. I have an aunt who is a washerwoman.'

'There, there,' said Toad, 'never mind; think no more about it. *I* have several aunts who *ought* to be washerwomen.'

'Do be quiet a minute, Toad,' said the girl. 'You talk too much, that's your chief fault, and I'm trying to think, and you hurt my head. As I said, I have an aunt who is a washerwoman; she does the washing for all the prisoners in this castle. She takes out the washing on Monday morning, and brings it in on Friday evening. This is a Thursday. Now, this is what occurs to me: you're very rich – at least you're always telling me so – and she's very poor. A few pounds wouldn't make any difference to you, and it would mean a lot to her. Now, I think if she were properly approached you could come to some arrangement by which she would let you have her dress and bonnet and so on, and you could escape from the castle as the official washerwoman. You're very alike in many respects – particularly about the figure.'

'We're *not*,' said the Toad in a huff.

'I have a very elegant figure – for what I am.'

'So has my aunt,' replied the girl, 'for what *she* is. But have it your own way. You horrid, proud, ungrateful animal, when I'm sorry for you, and trying to help you!'

'Yes, yes, that's all right; thank you very much indeed,' said the Toad hurriedly. 'But look here! You wouldn't surely have Mr Toad, of Toad Hall, going about the country disguised as a washerwoman!'

'Then you can stop here as a toad,' replied the girl with much spirit. 'I suppose you want to go off in a horse-driven coach!'

Honest Toad was always ready to admit himself in the wrong. 'You are a good, kind, clever girl,' he said, 'and I am indeed a proud and a stupid toad. Introduce me to your worthy aunt, if you will be so kind, and I have no doubt that the excellent lady and I will be able to arrange terms satisfactory to both parties.'

Next evening the girl took her aunt into Toad's cell, bearing his week's washing pinned up in a towel. The old lady had been prepared beforehand for the interview, and the sight of certain golden coins that Toad had thoughtfully

placed on the table in full view practically completed the matter and left little further to discuss. In return for his cash, Toad received a cotton print gown, an apron, a shawl, and a black bonnet; the only demand the old lady made was that she should be gagged and bound and dumped down in a corner. By this trick, she explained, no one would think she had helped Toad escape.

Toad was delighted with the suggestion. It would enable him to leave the prison in some style, and with his reputation for being a desperate and dangerous fellow unharmed; and he readily helped the jailer's daughter to make her aunt appear as much as possible the victim of circumstances over which she had no control.

'Now it's your turn, Toad,' said the girl. 'Take off that coat and waistcoat of yours; you're fat enough as it is.'

Shaking with laughter, she proceeded to dress him in the cotton print gown, arranged the shawl around him, and tied the strings of the bonnet under his chin.

'You're the very image of her,' she giggled, 'only I'm sure you never looked half so respectable in all your life before. Now, goodbye, Toad, and good luck. Go straight down the way you came up; and if anyone says anything to you, as they probably will, being but men, you can answer back a bit, of course, but remember you're a widow woman, quite alone in the world.'

With a quaking heart, but as firm a footstep as he could command, Toad set forth; but he was soon agreeably surprised to find how easy everything was made for him. The washerwoman's dumpy figure in its familiar cotton print seemed a passport for every barred door and grim gateway;

even when he hesitated, uncertain as to the right turning to take, he found himself helped out of his difficulty by the warder at the next gate, anxious to be off to his tea.

It seemed hours before he crossed the last courtyard, rejected the pressing invitations from the last guardroom, and dodged the outspread arms of the last warder, pleading for just one farewell embrace. But at last he heard the wicket-gate in the great outer door click behind him, felt the fresh air of the outer world upon his brow, and knew that he was free!

Dizzy with the easy success of his daring exploit, he walked quickly towards the lights of the town, not knowing in the least what he should do next, only quite certain of one thing, that he must remove himself as quickly as possible from the neighbourhood.

As he walked along, considering, his attention was caught by some red and green lights a little way off, to one side of the town, and the sound of the puffing and snorting of engines, and the banging of shunted trucks fell on his ear. 'Aha!' he thought. 'This is a piece of luck! A railway station is the thing I want most in the whole world at this moment.'

He made his way to the station, looked at a timetable, and found that a train, bound more or less in the direction of his home, was due to start in half an hour. 'More luck!' said Toad, his spirits rising rapidly, and went off to the booking office to buy his ticket.

He gave the name of the station that he knew to be nearest to Toad Hall and put his fingers, in search of the necessary money, where his waistcoat pocket should have been. But here the cotton gown, which had nobly stood by him so far, frustrated his efforts. In a sort of nightmare he struggled with the strange thing that seemed to hold his hands and laugh at him all the time; while other travellers, forming up in a line behind, waited with impatience, making suggestions of more or less value. At last, somehow, he never rightly understood how, he burst the barriers, arrived at where all waistcoat pockets are always situated, and found not only no money, but no pocket to hold it, and no waistcoat to hold the pocket!

To his horror he remembered that he had left both coat and waistcoat behind him in his cell, and with them his pocket book, money, keys, watch, matches, pencil case; all that makes life worth living, all that sets the many-pocketed animal above the inferior one-pocketed or no-pocketed types.

In his misery he made one desperate effort to carry the thing off, and, with a return to his fine old manner, he said, 'Look here! I find I've left my purse behind. Just give me that ticket, will you, and I'll send the money on tomorrow. I'm well known in these parts.'

The clerk stared at him and the black bonnet a moment, and then laughed. 'I should think you were pretty well known in these parts,' he said, 'if you've tried this game on often. Here, stand away from the window, please, madam; you're blocking the other passengers!'

An old gentleman who had been prodding him in the back for some moments here thrust him away, and, what was worse, addressed him as his good woman, which angered Toad more than anything that had happened that evening.

Baffled and full of despair, he wandered blindly down the platform where the train was standing, and tears trickled down each side of his nose. It was hard, he thought, to be within sight of safety and almost of home, and to be beaten by not having any money. Very soon his escape would be discovered, the hunt would be up, he would be caught, loaded with chains, dragged back again to prison, and bread and water and straw; and O, what sarcastic remarks the girl would make! What was to be done? He was not swift of foot; his figure was unfortunately recognisable. Could he not squeeze under the seat of a carriage? He had seen this method used by schoolboys, when the journey money provided by thoughtful parents had been diverted to other and better ends. As he pondered, he found himself opposite the engine, which was being oiled and wiped by its affectionate driver, a burly man with an oil-can in one hand and a lump of rag in the other.

'Hullo, mother!' said the engine driver. 'What's the trouble? You don't look particularly cheerful.'

'O, sir!' said Toad, crying afresh. 'I am a poor unhappy washerwoman, and I've lost all my money, and can't pay for a ticket, and I *must* get home tonight somehow, and whatever I am to do I don't know. O dear, O dear!'

'That's a bad business, indeed,' said the engine driver. 'Lost your money and can't get home, and got some kids, too, waiting for you, I dare say?'

'Any amount of 'em,' sobbed Toad. 'And they'll be hungry, and playing with matches, and upsetting lamps, the little innocents! And quarrelling, and going on generally. O dear, O dear!'

'Well, I'll tell you what I'll do,' said the good engine driver. 'You're a washerwoman to your trade, says you. Very well, that's that. And I'm an engine driver, as you well may see, and there's no denying it's terribly dirty work. Uses up a power of shirts, it does, till my missus is fair tired of washing 'em. If you'll wash a few shirts for me when you get home, and send 'em along, I'll give you a ride on my engine. It's against the Company's regulations, but we're not so very particular in these out-of-the-way parts.'

The Toad's misery turned into rapture as he eagerly scrambled up into the cab of the engine. Of course, he had never washed a shirt in his life, and couldn't if he tried and, anyhow, he wasn't going to begin; but he thought: 'When I get safely home to Toad Hall, and have money again, and pockets to put it in, I will send the engine driver enough to pay for quite a quantity of washing, and that will be the same thing, or better.'

The guard waved his welcome flag, the engine driver whistled, and the train moved out of the station. As the speed increased, and the Toad could see on either side of him real fields, and trees, and hedges, and cows, and horses, all flying past him, and as he thought how every minute was bringing him nearer to Toad Hall, and sympathetic friends, and money to chink in his pocket, and a soft bed to sleep in, and good things to eat, and praise and admiration at the recital of his adventures and his cleverness, he began to skip up and down and shout and sing snatches of song, to the great astonishment of the engine driver, who had come across washerwomen before, but never one at all like this.

They had covered many and many a mile, and Toad was already considering what he would have for supper as soon as he got home, when he noticed that the engine driver, with a puzzled expression on his face, was leaning over the side of the engine and listening hard. Then he saw him climb on to the coals and gaze out over the top of the train; then he returned and said to Toad: 'It's very strange; we're the last train running in this direction tonight, yet I could have sworn that I heard another following us!'

Toad stopped his antics at once. He became grave and depressed, and a dull pain in the lower part of his spine, moving down to his legs, made him want to sit down and try desperately not to think of what might happen.

By this time the moon was shining brightly, and the engine driver, steadying himself on the coal, could see the line behind them for a long distance.

Presently he called out, 'I can see it clearly now! It is an engine, on our rails, coming along at a great speed! It looks as if we are being followed!'

The miserable Toad, crouching in the coal dust, tried hard to think of something to do, with dismal lack of success.

'They are gaining on us fast!' cried the engine driver. 'And the engine is crowded with the queerest lot of people! Men like ancient warders; policemen in their helmets, waving truncheons; and shabbily dressed men in pot hats, unmistakable plain-clothes detectives even at this distance, waving revolvers and walking-sticks; all waving, and all shouting the same thing – "Stop, stop, stop!"'

Then Toad fell on his knees among the coals and, raising his clasped paws in prayer, cried, 'Save me, only save me, dear kind Mr Engine Driver, and I will confess everything! I am not the simple washerwoman I seem to be! I have no children waiting for me. I am a toad: the well-known and popular Mr Toad;

I have just escaped, by my great daring and cleverness, from a dungeon into which my enemies had flung me; and if those fellows on that engine recapture me, it will be chains and bread and water and straw and misery once more for poor, unhappy, innocent Toad!'

The engine driver looked down upon him very sternly, and said, 'Now tell the truth; what were you put in prison for?'

'It was nothing very much,' said poor Toad, blushing deeply. 'I only borrowed a motor-car while the owners were at lunch; they had no need of it at the time. I didn't mean to steal it, really; but people, especially magistrates, take such harsh views of thoughtless and high spirited actions.'

The engine driver looked very grave and said, 'I fear that you have been indeed a wicked toad, and by rights I ought to give you up. But you are evidently in trouble and distress, so I will not desert you. I don't hold with motor-cars, for one thing; and I don't hold with being ordered about by policemen when I'm on my own engine, for another. And the sight of an animal in tears always makes me feel soft-hearted. So cheer up, Toad! I'll do my best, and we may beat them yet!'

They piled on more coals, shovelling furiously; the furnace roared, the sparks flew, the engine leapt and swung, but still the other engine slowly gained. The engine driver, with a sigh, wiped his brow with a rag, and said, 'I'm afraid it's no good, Toad. You see, they are running light, and they have the better engine. There's just one thing left for us to do, and it's your only chance, so listen very carefully to what I tell you. A short way ahead of us is a long tunnel, and on the other side of that the line passes through a thick wood. Now, I will put on all the speed I can while we are running through the tunnel, but the other fellows will slow down a bit, for fear of an accident. When we are through, I will shut off steam and put on brakes as hard as I can, and the moment it's safe to do so you must jump and hide in the wood, before they get through the tunnel and see you. Then I will go full speed ahead again, and they can chase *me* if they like, for as long as they like, and as far as they like. Now mind and be ready to jump when I tell you!'

They piled on more coals, and the train shot into the tunnel, and the engine rushed and roared and rattled, till at last they shot out at the other end into fresh air and the peaceful moonlight, and saw the wood lying dark and helpful upon either side of the line. The driver shut off steam and put on brakes, the Toad got down on the step, and as the train slowed down to almost a walking pace he heard the driver call out, 'Now, jump!'

Toad jumped, rolled down a short bank, picked himself up unhurt, scrambled into the wood and hid.

Peeping out, he saw his train get up speed again and disappear at a great pace. Then out of the tunnel burst the other engine, roaring and whistling, her motley crew waving their various weapons and shouting, 'Stop! Stop! Stop!' When they were past, the Toad had a hearty laugh for the first time since he was thrown into prison.

But he soon stopped laughing when he came to consider that it was now very late and dark and cold, and he was in an unknown wood, with no money and no chance of supper, and still far from friends and home; and the dead silence of everything, after the roar and rattle of the train, was something of a shock. He dared not leave the shelter of the trees, so he marched into the wood, with the idea of leaving the railway as far as possible behind him.

After so many weeks within walls, he found the wood strange and unfriendly. Nightjars, sounding their mechanical rattle, made him think that the wood was full of searching warders, closing in on him. An owl, swooping noiselessly towards him, brushed his shoulder with its wing, making him jump with the horrid certainty that it was a hand; then flitted off, moth-like, laughing its low *ho! ho! ho!* which Toad thought in very poor taste. Once he met a fox, who stopped, looked him up and down in a sarcastic sort of way, and said, 'Hullo, washerwoman! Half a pair of socks and a pillowcase short this week! Mind it doesn't occur again!' and swaggered off, sniggering. Toad looked about for a stone to throw at him, but could not succeed in finding one, which annoyed him more than anything. At last, cold, hungry, and tired out, he sought the shelter of a hollow tree, where with branches and dead leaves he made himself as comfortable a bed as he could, and slept soundly till the morning.

CHAPTER 8

The Further Adventures of Toad

THE front door of the hollow tree faced eastwards, so Toad was called at an early hour, partly by the bright sunlight streaming in on him, partly by the coldness of his toes, which made him dream that he was at home in bed in his own handsome room with the Tudor window, on a cold winter's night, and his bedclothes had got up, grumbling and protesting they couldn't stand the cold any longer, and had run downstairs to the kitchen fire to warm themselves; and he had followed, on bare feet, along miles and miles of icy stone-paved passages, arguing and pleading with them to be reasonable. He would probably have been awakened much earlier, had he not slept for some weeks on straw over stone flags, and almost forgotten the friendly feeling of thick blankets pulled well up round the chin.

Sitting up, he rubbed his eyes first and his complaining toes next, wondered for a moment where he was, looking round for familiar stone wall and little barred window; then, with a leap of the heart, remembered everything: his escape, his flight, his pursuit; remembered, first and best thing of all, that he was free!

He shook himself and brushed the dry leaves out of his clothes with his fingers; and, his grooming complete, marched forth into the comfortable morning sun, cold but confident, hungry but hopeful, all nervous terrors of yesterday dispelled by rest and sleep and heartening sunshine.

He had the world all to himself, that early summer morning. The dewy woodland, as he threaded his way through it, was solitary and still; the green fields that succeeded the trees were his own to do as he liked with; the road itself, when he reached it, in that loneliness that was everywhere, seemed, like a stray dog, to be looking for company. Toad, however, was looking for something that could talk, and tell him clearly which way he

ought to go. It is all very well, when you have a light heart, and a clear conscience, and money in your pocket, and nobody scouring the country for you to drag you off to prison again, to follow where the road beckons and points, not caring where. The practical Toad cared very much indeed, and he could have kicked the road for its helpless silence when every minute was of importance to him.

The road was presently joined by a canal which ambled along by its side. Round a bend in the canal came plodding a solitary horse, stooping forward as if in anxious thought. From rope traces attached to his collar stretched a long line, taut, but dipping with his stride, the further part of it dripping pearly drops. Toad let the horse pass, and stood waiting for what the fates were sending him.

With a pleasant swirl of quiet water at its blunt bow a barge slid up alongside of him, its gaily painted gunwale level with the towing path, its sole occupant a big stout woman wearing a linen sun bonnet, one brawny arm laid along the tiller.

'A nice morning, ma'am!' she remarked to Toad, as she drew up level with him.

'I dare say it is, ma'am!' responded Toad politely, as he walked along the towpath abreast of her. 'I dare say it is a nice morning to them that's not in sore trouble, like what I am. Here's my married daughter, she sends off to me post haste to come to her at once; so off I comes, not knowing what may be happening or going to happen, but fearing the worst, as you will understand, ma'am, if you're a mother, too. And I've left my business to look after itself, I'm in the washing and laundering line, you must know, ma'am, and I've left

…106…

my young children to look after themselves, and a more mischievous and troublesome set of young imps doesn't exist, ma'am; and I've lost all my money, and lost my way, and as for what may be happening to my married daughter, why, I don't like to think of it, ma'am!'

'Where might your married daughter be living, ma'am?' asked the barge woman.

'She lives near to the river, ma'am,' replied Toad. 'Close to a fine house called Toad Hall, that's somewhere hereabouts in these parts. Perhaps you may have heard of it.'

'Toad Hall? Why, I'm going that way myself,' replied the barge woman. 'This canal joins the river some miles further on, a little above Toad Hall; and then it's an easy walk. You come along in the barge with me, and I'll give you a lift.'

She steered the barge close to the bank, and Toad, with many humble thanks, stepped lightly on board and sat down with great satisfaction. *Toad's luck again!* thought he. *I always come out on top!*

'So you're in the washing business, ma'am?' said the barge woman politely, as they glided along. 'And a very good business you've got too, I dare say, if I'm not making too free in saying so.'

'Finest business in the whole county,' said Toad airily. 'All the gentry come to me: wouldn't go to anyone else if they were paid, they know me so well. You see, I understand my work thoroughly, and attend to it all myself. Washing, ironing, clear-starching, making up gents' fine shirts for evening wear – everything's done under my own eye!'

'But surely you don't *do* all that work yourself, ma'am?' asked the barge woman respectfully.

'O, I have girls,' said Toad lightly. 'Twenty girls or thereabouts, always at work. But you know what *girls* are, ma'am! Nasty little hussies, that's what *I* call 'em!'

'So do I, too,' said the barge woman with great heartiness. 'But I dare say you set yours to rights, the lazy things! And are you *very* fond of washing?'

'I love it,' said Toad. 'I simply dote on it. Never so happy as when I've got both arms in the wash tub. But, then, it comes so easy to me! No trouble at all! A real pleasure, I assure you, ma'am!'

'What a bit of luck, meeting you!' said the barge woman thoughtfully. 'A regular piece of good fortune for both of us!'

'Why, what do you mean?' asked Toad nervously.

'Well, look at me, now,' replied the barge woman. 'I like washing, too, just the same as you do; and for that matter, whether I like it or not I have got to do all my own, naturally, moving about as I do. Now my husband, he's such a fellow for shirking his work and leaving the barge to me, never a moment do I get for seeing to my own affairs. By rights he ought to be here now, either steering or attending to the horse, though luckily the horse has sense enough to attend to himself. Instead of which, he's gone off with the dog, to see if they can't pick up a rabbit for dinner somewhere. Says he'll catch me up at the next lock. Well, that's as may be; I don't trust him, once he gets off with that dog, who's worse than he is. But, meantime, how am I to get on with my washing?'

'O, never mind about the washing,' said Toad, not liking the subject. 'Try and fix your mind on that rabbit. A nice fat young rabbit, I'll be bound. Got any onions?'

'I can't fix my mind on anything but my washing,' said the barge woman, 'and I wonder you can be talking of rabbits, with such a joyful prospect before you. There's a heap of things of mine that you'll find in a corner of the cabin. If you'll just take one or two of the most necessary sort

– I won't venture to describe them to a lady like you, but you'll recognise 'em at a glance – and put them through the wash tub as we go along. Why, it'll be a pleasure to you, as you rightly say, and a real help to me. You'll find a tub handy, and soap, and a kettle on the stove, and a bucket to haul up water from the canal with. Then I shall know you're enjoying yourself, instead of sitting here idle, looking at the scenery and yawning your head off.'

'Here, you let me steer,' said Toad, now thoroughly frightened, 'and then you can get on with your washing your own way. I might spoil your things, or not do 'em as you like. I'm more used to gentlemen's things myself. It's my special line.'

'Let you steer?' replied the barge woman, laughing. 'It takes some practice to steer a barge properly. Besides, it's dull work, and I want you to be happy. No, you shall do the washing you are so fond of, and I'll stick to the steering that I understand. Don't try and deprive me of the pleasure of giving you a treat!'

Toad was fairly cornered. He looked for escape this way and that, saw that he was too far from the bank for a flying leap, and sullenly resigned himself to his fate. *If it comes to that*, he thought in desperation, *I suppose any fool can wash!*

He fetched tub, soap, and other necessaries from the cabin, selected a few garments at random, tried to recollect what he had seen in casual glances through laundry windows, and set to.

A long half-hour passed, and every minute of it saw Toad getting crosser and crosser. Nothing that he could do to the things seemed to please them or do them good. He tried coaxing, he tried slapping, he tried punching; they smiled back at him out of the tub unconverted. Once or twice he looked nervously over his shoulder at the barge woman, but she appeared to be gazing out in front of her, busy with her steering. His back ached badly, and he noticed with dismay that his paws were beginning to get all crinkly. Now Toad was very proud of his paws. He muttered under his breath words that should never pass the lips of either washerwomen or toads; and lost the soap, for the fiftieth time.

A burst of laughter made him straighten himself and look round. The barge woman was leaning back and laughing, till the tears ran down her cheeks.

'I've been watching you all the time,' she gasped. 'I thought you must be a humbug all along, from the conceited way you talked. Pretty washerwoman you are! Never washed so much as a dish cloth in your life, I'd say!'

Toad's temper, which had been simmering viciously for some time, now fairly boiled over, and he lost all control of himself.

'You common, low, *fat* barge woman!' he shouted. 'Don't you dare to talk to your betters like that! Washerwoman indeed! I would have you to know that I am a Toad, a very well-known, respected, distinguished Toad! I may be under a bit of a cloud at present, but I will *not* be laughed at by a barge woman!'

The woman moved nearer to him and peered under his bonnet keenly and closely. 'Why, so you are!' she cried. 'Well, I never! A horrid, nasty, crawly Toad! And in my nice clean barge, too! Now that is a thing that I will *not* have.'

She let go of the tiller for a moment. One big mottled arm shot out and caught Toad by a foreleg, while the other gripped him fast by a hindleg. Then the world turned suddenly upside down, the wind whistled in his ears, and Toad found himself flying through the air, revolving rapidly as he went.

The water, when he eventually reached it with a loud splash, proved quite cold enough for his taste, though its chill was not sufficient to quell his proud spirit, or slake the heat of his furious temper. He rose to the surface spluttering, and when he had wiped the duckweed out of his eyes the first thing he saw was the fat barge woman looking back at him over the stern of the barge and laughing; and he vowed, as he coughed and choked, to be even with her.

He struck out for the shore, but the cotton gown impeded his efforts, and when at length he touched land he found it hard to climb up the steep bank. He had to take a minute or two's rest to recover his breath; then, gathering his wet skirts well over his arms, he started to run after the barge as fast as his legs would carry him, wild with indignation, thirsting for revenge.

The barge woman was still laughing when he drew up level with her. 'Put yourself through your mangle, washerwoman,' she called out, 'and iron your face and crimp it, and you'll pass for quite a decent looking Toad!'

Toad never paused to reply. Revenge was what he wanted, not an exchange of words, though he had a thing or two in his mind that he would have liked to say. He saw what he wanted ahead of him. Running swiftly on he overtook the horse, unfastened the tow rope and cast off, jumped lightly on the horse's back, and urged it to a gallop by kicking it hard in the sides. He steered for the open country, leaving the tow path, and swinging his steed down a bumpy lane. Once he looked back, and saw that the barge had run aground on the other side of the canal, and the barge woman was waving her arms wildly and shouting, 'Stop, stop, stop!' 'I've heard that song before,' said Toad, laughing, as he continued to spur his steed onward in its wild gallop.

The barge horse was not capable of any very sustained effort, and its gallop soon subsided into a trot, and its trot into an easy walk; but Toad was quite contented with this, knowing that he, at any rate, was moving, and the barge was not. He had quite recovered his temper, now that he had done something he thought really clever; and he was satisfied to jog along quietly in the sun, taking advantage of any byways and bridle-paths, and trying to forget how very long it was since he had

had a square meal, till the canal had been left very far behind him.

He had travelled some miles, his horse and he, and he was feeling drowsy in the hot sunshine, when the horse stopped, lowered his head, and began to nibble the grass; and Toad, waking up, just saved himself from falling off by an effort. He looked about him and found he was on a wide common, dotted with patches of gorse and bramble as far as he could see. Near him stood a dingy gipsy caravan, and beside it a man was sitting on a bucket turned upside down, very busy smoking and staring into the wide world. A fire of sticks was burning near by, and over the fire hung an iron pot, and out of that pot came forth bubblings and gurglings. Also smells: warm, rich, and varied smells, that twined and twisted and wreathed themselves at last into one complete, perfect smell. Toad now knew well that he had not been really hungry before. What he had felt earlier in the day had been nothing. This was the real thing at last, and no mistake; and it would have to be dealt with speedily, too, or there would be trouble for somebody or something. He looked the gipsy over carefully, wondering whether it would be easier to fight him or speak nicely to him. So there he sat, and sniffed and sniffed, and looked at the gipsy; and the gipsy sat and smoked, and looked at him.

Presently the gipsy took his pipe out of his mouth and remarked in a careless way, 'Want to sell that horse of yours?'

Toad was completely taken aback. He did not know that gipsies were very fond of horse-dealing, and never missed an opportunity, and he had not reflected that caravans were always on the move and took a deal of drawing. It had not occurred to him to turn the horse into cash, but the gipsy's suggestion seemed to smooth the way towards the two things he wanted: ready money and a solid breakfast.

'What?' he said. 'Me sell this beautiful young horse of mine? O no; it's out of the question. Who's going to take the washing home to my customers every week? Besides, I'm too fond of him, and he simply dotes on me.'

'Try and love a donkey,' suggested the gipsy. 'Some people do.'

'You don't seem to see,' continued Toad, 'that this fine horse of mine is a cut above you altogether. He's a blood horse, he is, partly; not the part you see, of course, another part. And he's been a Prize Hackney, too, in his time, that was the time before you knew him, but you can still tell it on him at a glance if you understand anything about horses. No, it's not to be thought of for a moment. All the same, how much would you offer me for this beautiful young horse of mine?'

The gipsy looked the horse over, and then he looked Toad over with equal care, and looked at the horse again.

'Shillin' a leg,' he said briefly, and turned away.

'A shilling a leg?' cried Toad. 'If you please, I must take a little time to work that out, and see just what it comes to.'

He climbed down off his horse, and left it to graze, and sat down by the gipsy, and did sums on his fingers, and at last he said, 'A shilling a leg? Why, that comes to exactly four shillings, and no more. O no; I could not think of accepting four shillings for this beautiful young horse of mine.'

'Well,' said the gipsy, 'I'll tell you what I will do. I'll make it five shillings, and that's three-and-sixpence more than the animal's worth. And that's my last word.'

Then Toad sat and pondered long and deeply. For he was hungry and quite penniless, and still some way, he knew not how far, from home, and enemies might still be looking for him. To one in such a situation, five shillings may very well appear a large sum of money. On the other hand, it did not seem very much to get for a horse. But then, again, the horse hadn't cost him anything; so whatever he got was all clear profit. At last he said firmly, 'Look here, gipsy! I tell you what we will do; and this is *my* last word. You shall hand me over six shillings and sixpence, cash down; and in addition you shall give me as much breakfast as I can possibly eat, at one sitting of course, out of that iron pot of yours that keeps sending forth such delicious and exciting smells. In return, I will make over to you my spirited young horse, with all the beautiful harness and

trappings that are on him, freely thrown in. If that's not good enough for you, say so, and I'll be getting on. I know a man near here who's wanted this horse of mine for years.'

The gipsy grumbled, and declared if he did a few more deals of that sort he'd be ruined. But in the end he lugged a dirty canvas bag out of the depths of his trouser pocket, and counted out six shillings and sixpence into Toad's paw. Then he disappeared into the caravan for an instant, and returned with a large iron plate and a knife, fork, and spoon. He tilted up the pot, and a glorious stream of hot rich stew gurgled into the plate. It was, indeed, the most beautiful stew in the world, being made of partridges, and pheasants, and chickens, and hares, and rabbits, and peahens, and guinea fowls, and one or two other things. Toad took the plate on his lap, almost crying, and stuffed, and stuffed, and stuffed, and kept asking for more, and the gipsy never grudged it him. He thought that he had never eaten so good a breakfast in all his life.

When Toad had taken as much stew on board as he thought he could possibly hold, he got up and said goodbye to the gipsy, and took an affectionate farewell of the horse; and the gipsy, who knew the riverside well, gave him directions which way to go, and he set forth on his travels again in the best possible spirits. He was, indeed, a very different Toad from the animal of an hour ago. The sun was shining brightly, his wet clothes were quite dry again, he had money in his pockets once more, he was nearing home and friends and safety, and, most and best of all, he had had a substantial meal, hot and nourishing, and felt big, and strong, and careless, and self-confident.

As he tramped along gaily, he thought of his adventures and escapes, and how when things seemed at their worst he had always managed to find a way out; and his pride and conceit began to swell within him. 'Ho, ho!' he said to himself as he marched along with his chin in the air, 'what a clever Toad I am! There is surely no animal equal to me for cleverness in the whole world! Ho, ho! I am The Toad, the handsome, the popular, the successful Toad!' He got so puffed up with conceit that he made up a song as he walked in praise of himself, and sang it at the top of his voice, though there was no one to hear it but him. It was perhaps the most conceited song that any animal ever composed:

> The world has held great Heroes,
> As history books have showed;
> But never a name to go down to fame
> Compared with that of Toad!
>
> The clever men at Oxford
> Know all that there is to be knowed.
> But they none of them know one half as much
> As intelligent Mr Toad!
>
> The animals sat in the Ark and cried,
> Their tears in torrents flowed.

Who was it said, 'There's land ahead'?
Encouraging Mr Toad!

The Army all saluted
As they marched along the road.
Was it the King? Or Kitchener?
No! It was Mr Toad!

The Queen and her ladies-in-waiting
Sat at the window and sewed.
She cried, 'Look! Who's that
handsome man?'
They answered, 'Mr Toad!

He sang as he walked, and he walked as he
sang, and got more inflated every minute. But his
pride was shortly to have a severe fall.

After some miles of country lanes he reached the high road, and as he
turned into it and glanced along its white length, he saw approaching him
a speck that turned into a dot and then into a blob, and then into
something very familiar; and a double note of warning, only too well known,
fell on his delighted ear.

'This is something splendid!' said the excited Toad. 'This is real life again,
this is once more the great world from which I have been missed so long!
I will hail them, my brothers of the wheel, and pitch them a yarn, of the
sort that has been so successful up to now; and they will give me a lift,
of course, and then I will talk to them some more; and, perhaps, with luck,
it may even end in my driving up to Toad Hall in a motor-car! That will be
one in the eye for Badger!'

He stepped confidently out into the road to hail the motor-car, which
came along at an easy pace, slowing down as it neared the lane; when
suddenly he became very pale, his heart turned to water, his knees shook,

and he doubled up and collapsed with a sickening pain in his insides. And well he might, the unhappy animal; for the approaching car was the very one he had stolen out of the yard of the Red Lion Hotel on that fatal day when all his troubles began! And the people in it were the very same people he had sat and watched at lunch in the coffee room!

He sank down in a shabby, miserable heap in the road, murmuring to himself in his despair, 'It's all up! It's all over now! Chains and policemen again! Prison again! Dry bread and water again! O, what a fool I have been! What did I want to go strutting about the country for, singing conceited songs, and hailing people in broad daylight on the high road, instead of hiding till nightfall and slipping home quietly by back ways? O hapless Toad! O ill-fated animal!'

The terrible motor-car drew slowly nearer and nearer, till at last he heard it stop just short of him. Two gentlemen got out and walked round the trembling heap of crumpled misery lying in the road, and one of them said, 'O dear! This is very sad! Here is a poor old thing, a washerwoman apparently, who has fainted in the road! Perhaps she is overcome by the heat, poor creature; or possibly she has not had any food today. Let us lift her into the car and take her to the nearest village, where doubtless she has friends.'

They tenderly lifted Toad into the motor-car and propped him up with soft cushions, and went on their way.

When Toad heard them talk in so kind and sympathetic a manner, he knew that he was not recognised, his courage began to revive, and he cautiously opened first one eye and then the other.

'Look!' said one of the gentlemen. 'She is better already. The fresh air is doing her good. How do you feel now, ma'am?'

'Thank you kindly, sir,' said Toad in a feeble voice. 'I'm feeling a great deal better!'

'That's right,' said the gentleman. 'Now keep quite still, and, above all, don't try to talk.'

'I won't,' said Toad. 'I was only thinking, if I might sit on the front seat there, beside the driver, where I could get the fresh air full in my face, I should soon be all right again.'

'What a very sensible woman!' said the gentleman. 'Of course you shall.' So they carefully helped Toad into the front seat beside the driver, and on they went once more.

Toad was almost himself again by now. He sat up, looked about him, and tried to be calm.

'It is fate!' he said to himself. 'Why strive? Why struggle?' and he turned to the driver at his side. 'Please, sir,' he said, 'I wish you would kindly let me try and drive the car for a little. I've been watching you carefully, and it looks so easy and so interesting, and I should like to be able to tell my friends that once I had driven a motor-car!'

The driver laughed at the proposal, so heartily that the gentleman asked what the matter was. When he heard, he said, to Toad's delight, 'Bravo, ma'am! I like your spirit. Let her have a try, and look after her. She won't do any harm.'

Toad eagerly scrambled into the driver's seat, took the steering wheel in his hands, listened with affected humility to the instructions given him, and very slowly and carefully, he set the car in motion.

The gentlemen behind clapped their hands and applauded, and Toad heard them saying, 'How well she does it! Fancy a washerwoman driving a car as well as that, the first time!'

Toad went a little faster; then faster still, and faster.

He heard the gentleman call out warningly, 'Be careful, washerwoman!' This annoyed him, and he began to lose his head.

The driver tried to interfere, but he pinned him down in his seat with one elbow, and put on full speed. The rush of air in his face, the hum of the engine, and the light jump of the car beneath him made him very excited.

'Washerwoman, indeed!' he shouted recklessly. 'Ho, ho! I am the Toad, the motor-car snatcher, the prison-breaker, the Toad who always escapes! Sit still, and you shall know what driving really is, for you are in the hands of the famous, the skilful, the entirely fearless Toad!'

With a cry of horror the whole party rose and flung themselves on him. 'Seize him!' they cried. 'Seize the Toad, the wicked animal who stole our motor car! Bind him, chain him, drag him to the nearest police station! Down with the desperate and dangerous Toad!'

Alas! They should have thought, they should have remembered to stop the motor-car somehow before playing any pranks of that sort. With a half turn of the wheel the Toad sent the car crashing through the low hedge that ran along the roadside. One mighty bound, a violent shock, and the wheels of the car were churning up the thick mud of a horse pond.

Toad found himself flying through the air with the strong upward rush and delicate curve of a swallow. He liked the motion, and was just beginning to wonder whether it would go on, when he landed on his back with a thump, in the soft rich grass of a meadow. Sitting up, he could just see the motor-car in the pond, nearly submerged; the gentlemen and the driver, weighed down by their long coats, were floundering helplessly in the water.

He picked himself up rapidly and set off running across country as hard as he could, scrambling through hedges, jumping ditches, pounding across fields, till he was breathless and weary, and had to settle down into an easy walk. When he had recovered his breath somewhat, and was able to think calmly, he began to giggle, and from giggling he took to laughing, and he laughed till he had to sit down under a hedge. 'Ho, ho!' he cried. 'Toad again! Toad, as usual, comes out on the top! Who was it got them to give him a lift? Who managed to get on the front seat for the sake of fresh air? Who persuaded them into letting him see if he could drive? Who landed them all in a horse pond? Who escaped, flying gaily and unhurt through the air, leaving all of them in the mud where they should rightly be? Why, Toad, of course; clever Toad, great Toad, *good* Toad!'

Then he burst into song again, and chanted with uplifted voice:

> The motor-car went Poop-poop-poop,
> As it raced along the road.
> Who was it steered it into a pond?
> Ingenious Mr Toad!

'O, how clever I am! How clever, how clever, how very clev –'

A slight noise at a distance behind him made him turn his head and look. O horror! O misery! O despair!

About two fields off, a chauffeur in his leather gaiters and two large rural policemen were visible, running towards him as hard as they could go!

Poor Toad sprang to his feet and pelted away again, his heart in his mouth. 'O my!' he gasped, as he panted along. 'What a fool I am! What a *conceited* and heedless fool! Swaggering again! Shouting and singing songs again! Sitting still and gassing again! O my! O my! O my!'

He glanced back, and saw to his dismay that they were gaining on him. On he ran desperately, but kept looking back, and saw that they still gained steadily. He did his best, but he was a fat animal, and his legs were short, and still they gained. He could hear them close behind him now. Ceasing to heed where he was going, he struggled on blindly and wildly, looking back over his shoulder at the now triumphant enemy, when suddenly the earth failed under his feet, he grasped at the air, and, *splash*! he found himself head over ears in deep water, rapid water, water that bore him along with a force he could not contend with; and he knew that in his blind panic he had run straight into the river!

He rose to the surface and tried to grasp the reeds and the rushes that grew along the water's edge close under the bank, but the stream was so strong that it tore them out of his hands. 'O my!' gasped poor Toad. 'If ever I steal a motor-car again! If ever I sing another conceited song–' then down he went, and came up breathless and spluttering. Presently he saw that he was approaching a big dark hole in the bank, just above his head, and as the stream bore him past he reached up with a paw and caught hold of the edge and held on. Then slowly and with difficulty he drew himself up out of the water, till at last he was able to rest his elbows on the edge of the hole. There he remained for some minutes, puffing and panting, for he was quite exhausted.

As he sighed and blew and stared before him into the dark hole, some bright small thing shone and twinkled in its depths, moving towards him. As it approached, a face grew up gradually around it, and it was a familiar face!

Brown and small, with whiskers.

Grave and round, with neat ears and silky hair. It was the Water Rat!

CHAPTER 9

'Like Summer Tempests Came His Tears'

THE Rat put out a neat little brown paw, gripped Toad firmly by the scruff of the neck, and gave a great hoist and a pull; and the waterlogged Toad came up slowly but surely over the edge of the hole, till at last he stood safe and sound in the hall, streaked with mud and weed to be sure, and with the water streaming off him, but happy and high-spirited as of old, now that he found himself once more in the house of a friend, and he could lay aside a disguise that was unworthy of his position.

'O Ratty!' he cried. 'I've been through such times since I saw you last, you can't think! Such trials, such sufferings, and all so nobly borne! Then such escapes, such disguises, such tricks, and all so cleverly planned and carried out! Been in prison, got out of it, of course! Been thrown into a canal, swam ashore! Stole a horse, sold him for a large sum of money! Humbugged everybody – made 'em all do exactly what I wanted! O, I *am* a smart Toad, and no mistake! What do you think my last exploit was? Just hold on till I tell you.'

'Toad,' said the Water Rat, gravely and firmly, 'you go off upstairs at once, and take off that old cotton rag that looks as if it might formerly have belonged to some washerwoman, and clean yourself thoroughly, and put on some of my clothes, and try and come down looking like a gentleman if you *can*; for a more shabby, bedraggled, disreputable looking object than you are I never set eyes on in my whole life! Now, stop swaggering and arguing, and be off! I'll have something to say to you later!'

Toad was at first inclined to stop and do some talking back at him. He had had enough of being ordered about when he was in prison. However, he caught sight of himself in the mirror over the hat-stand, with the black bonnet perched rakishly over one eye, and he changed his mind and went very quickly and humbly upstairs to the Rat's dressing room. There he had a thorough wash and brush up, changed his clothes, and stood for a long time before the glass, looking at himself with pride and pleasure, and thinking what utter idiots all the people must have been to have ever mistaken him for one moment for a washerwoman.

By the time he came down again lunch was on the table, and very glad Toad was to see it, for he had been through some trying experiences and had taken much hard exercise since the excellent breakfast provided for him by the gipsy.

While they ate, Toad told the Rat all his adventures, dwelling chiefly on his own cleverness, and presence of mind in emergencies, and cunning in tight places. But the more he talked and boasted, the more grave and silent the Rat became.

When at last Toad had talked himself to a standstill, there was silence for a while; and then the Rat said, 'Now, Toady, I don't want to give you pain, after all you've been through already; but, seriously, don't you see what an awful idiot you've been making of yourself? On your own admission you have been handcuffed, imprisoned, starved, chased, terrified out of your life, insulted, jeered at, and shamefully flung into the water - by a woman, too! Where does the fun come in? And all because you must needs go and steal a motor-car. You know that you've never had anything but trouble from motor-cars from the moment you first set eyes on one. But if you *will* be mixed up with them as you generally are, five minutes after you've started, why *steal* them? Be a bankrupt, for a change, if you've set your mind on it; but why choose to be a convict? When are you going to be sensible, and think of your friends, and try and be a credit to them? Do you suppose it's any pleasure to me, for instance, to hear animals saying, as I go about, that I'm the fellow that keeps company with jail-birds?'

Now, it was a very comforting point in Toad's character that he was a thoroughly good-hearted animal, and never minded being told off by those who were his real friends. And even when most set upon a thing, he was always able to see the other side of the question. So although, while the Rat was talking so seriously, he kept saying to himself mutinously, 'But it *was* fun, though! Awful fun!' and making strange suppressed noises inside him, *k-i-ck-ck-ck*, and *poop-p-p*, and other sounds resembling stifled snorts, or the opening of soda-water bottles, yet when the Rat had quite finished, he heaved a deep sigh and said, very nicely and humbly, 'Quite right, Ratty! How *sound* you always are! Yes, I've been a conceited old fool, I can quite see that; but now I'm going to be a good Toad, and not do it any more. As for motor-cars, I've not been at all so keen about them since my last ducking in that river of yours. The fact is, while I was hanging on to the edge of your hole and getting my breath, I had a sudden idea, a really brilliant idea connected with motor-boats, there, there! Don't take on so and stamp, and upset things; it was only an idea, and we won't talk any more about it now. We'll have our coffee, *and* a smoke, and a quiet chat, and then I'm going to stroll gently down to Toad Hall, and get into clothes of my own, and set things going again on the old lines. I've had enough of adventures. I shall lead a quiet, steady, respectable life, pottering about my property, and improving it, and doing a little landscape gardening at times. There will always be a bit of dinner for my friends when they come to see me; and I shall keep a pony-carriage to jog about the country in, just as I used to in the good old days, before I got restless, and wanted to *do* things.'

'Stroll gently down to Toad Hall?' cried the Rat, greatly excited. 'What are you talking about? Do you mean to say you haven't *heard*?'

'Heard what?' said Toad, turning rather pale. 'Go on, Ratty! Quick! Don't spare me! What haven't I heard?'

'Do you mean to tell me,' shouted the Rat, thumping with his little fist upon the table, 'that you've heard nothing about the Stoats and Weasels?'

'What, the Wild Wooders?' cried Toad, trembling in every limb. 'No, not a word! What have they been doing?'

'And how they've been and taken Toad Hall?' continued the Rat.

Toad leaned his elbows on the table, and his chin on his paws; and a large tear welled up in each of his eyes, overflowed and splashed on the table, *plop! plop!*

'Go on, Ratty,' he murmured presently, 'tell me all. The worst is over. I am an animal again. I can bear it.'

'When you got into that trouble of yours,' said the Rat slowly and impressively, 'I mean, when you disappeared for a time, over that misunderstanding about a machine, you know.'

Toad merely nodded.

'Well, it was a good deal talked about down here, naturally,' continued the Rat, 'not only along the riverside, but even in the Wild Wood. Animals took sides, as always happens. The River Bankers stuck up for you, and said you had been wickedly treated, and there was no justice to be had in the land nowadays. But the Wild Wood animals said hard things, and that it served you right, and it was time this sort of thing was stopped. And they went about saying you were done for this time! You would never come back again, never, never!'

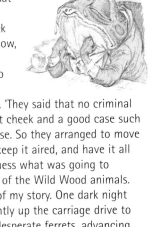

Toad nodded once more, keeping silent.

'That's the sort of little beasts they are,' the Rat went on. 'But Mole and Badger, they stuck out, through thick and thin, that you would come back again soon, somehow. They didn't know exactly how, but somehow!'

Toad began to sit up in his chair again, and to smirk a little.

'They argued from history,' continued the Rat. 'They said that no criminal laws had ever been known to win the day against cheek and a good case such as yours, combined with the power of a deep purse. So they arranged to move their things into Toad Hall, and sleep there, and keep it aired, and have it all ready for you when you turned up. They didn't guess what was going to happen, of course; still, they had their suspicions of the Wild Wood animals. Now I come to the most painful and tragic part of my story. One dark night a band of weasels, armed to the teeth, crept silently up the carriage drive to the front entrance. At the same time, a body of desperate ferrets, advancing through the kitchen garden, possessed themselves of the backyard and offices; while a company of skirmishing stoats who stopped at nothing occupied the conservatory and the billiard room, and held the French windows opening on to the lawn.

'The Mole and the Badger were sitting by the fire in the smoking room, telling stories and suspecting nothing, for it wasn't a night for any animals to be out in, when those bloodthirsty villains broke down the doors and rushed in upon them from every side. They made the best fight they could, but what was the good? They were unarmed, and taken by surprise, and what can two animals do against hundreds? They took and beat them severely with sticks, those two poor faithful creatures, and turned them out into the cold and the wet, with many insulting and uncalled-for remarks!'

Here the unfeeling Toad broke into a snigger, and then pulled himself together and tried to look particularly solemn.

'And the Wild Wooders have been living in Toad Hall ever since,' continued the Rat, 'and going on simply anyhow! Lying in bed half the day, and breakfast at all hours, and the place in such a mess. I'm told it's not fit to be seen! Eating your grub, and drinking your drink, and making bad jokes about you, and singing vulgar songs, about, well, about prisons, and magistrates, and policemen; horrid personal songs, with no humour in them. And they're telling the tradespeople and everybody that they've come to stay for good.'

'O, have they!' said Toad, getting up and seizing a stick. 'I'll soon see about that!'

'It's no good, Toad!' called the Rat after him. 'You'd better come back and sit down; you'll only get into trouble.'

But the Toad was off, and there was no holding him. He marched rapidly down the road, his stick over his shoulder, fuming and muttering to himself in his anger, till he got near his front gate, when suddenly there popped up from behind the palings a long yellow ferret with a gun.

'Who comes there?' said the ferret sharply.

'Stuff and nonsense!' said Toad very angrily. 'What do you mean by talking like that to me? Come out of it at once, or I'll...'

The ferret said never a word, but he brought his gun up to his shoulder. Toad dropped flat in the road, and *Bang!* a bullet whistled over his head.

The startled Toad scrambled to his feet and scampered off down the road as hard as he could; and as he ran he heard the ferret laughing, and other horrid thin little laughs taking it up and carrying on the sound.

He went back, very crestfallen, and told the Water Rat.

'What did I tell you?' said the Rat. 'It's no good. They've got sentries posted, and they are all armed. You must just wait.'

Still, Toad was not going to give in all at once. So he got out the boat, and set off rowing up the river to where the garden front of Toad Hall came down to the waterside.

Arriving within sight of his old home, he rested on his oars and looked around carefully. All seemed very peaceful and deserted and quiet. He could see the whole front of Toad Hall glowing in the evening sunshine, the pigeons settling by twos and threes along the straight line of the roof; the garden, a blaze of flowers; the creek that led up to the boat house, the little wooden bridge that crossed it; all tranquil, uninhabited, apparently waiting for his return. He would try the boat house first, he thought. Very warily he paddled up to the mouth of the creek, and was just passing under the bridge, when... *Crash!*

A great stone, dropped from above, smashed through the bottom of the boat. It filled and sank, and Toad found himself struggling in deep water.

Looking up, he saw two stoats leaning over the bridge and watching him with great glee. 'It will be your head next time, Toady!' they called out to him. The indignant Toad swam to shore, while the stoats laughed and laughed.

The Toad retraced his weary way on foot, and related his disappointing experiences to the Water Rat once more.

'Well, *what* did I tell you?' said the Rat very crossly. 'And, now, look here! See what you've been and done! Lost me my boat that I was so fond of, that's what you've done! And simply ruined that nice suit of clothes that I lent you! Really, Toad, of all the trying animals – I wonder you manage to keep any friends at all!'

The Toad saw at once how wrongly and foolishly he had acted. He admitted his errors and made a full apology to Rat for losing his boat and spoiling his clothes. And he wound up by saying, 'Ratty! I see that I have been a headstrong and a wilful Toad! Henceforth, believe me, I will be humble and submissive, and will take no action without your kind advice and full approval!'

'If that is really so,' said the good-natured Rat, 'then my advice to you is, considering the lateness of the hour, to sit down and have your supper, which will be on the table in a minute, and be very patient. For I am convinced that we can do nothing until we have seen the Mole and the Badger, and heard their latest news, and held conference and taken their advice in this difficult matter.'

'O, ah, yes, of course, the Mole and the Badger,' said Toad lightly. 'What's become of them, the dear fellows? I had forgotten all about them.'

'Well may you ask!' said the Rat sharply. 'While you were riding about the country in expensive motor-cars, and galloping proudly on horses, and breakfasting on the fat of the land, those two poor devoted animals have been camping out in the open, in every sort of weather, living very rough

by day and lying very hard by night; watching over your house, keeping constant eye on the stoats and the weasels, scheming and planning how to get your property back for you. You don't deserve to have such true and loyal friends, Toad, you don't, really. Some day, when it's too late, you'll be sorry you didn't value them more while you had them!'

'I'm an ungrateful beast, I know,' sobbed Toad, shedding bitter tears. 'Let me go out and find them, out into the cold, dark night and share their hardships, and try and prove by – Hold on a bit! Surely I heard the chink of dishes on a tray! Supper's here at last, hooray! Come on, Ratty!'

The Rat remembered that poor Toad had been on prison rations for a considerable time, and that large allowances had therefore to be made. He followed him to the table and encouraged him in his gallant efforts to make up for past hardships.

They had just finished their meal and returned to their armchairs, when there came a heavy knock at the door.

Toad was nervous, but the Rat, nodding mysteriously at him, went straight up to the door and opened it, and in walked Mr Badger.

He had all the appearance of one who for some nights had been kept away from home and all its little comforts and conveniences. His shoes were covered with mud, and he was looking very rough and untidy; but then he had never been a very smart man, the Badger, at the best of times. He came solemnly up to Toad, shook him by the paw, and said, 'Welcome home, Toad! Alas! What am I saying? Home, indeed! This is a poor homecoming. Unhappy Toad!' Then he turned his back on him, sat down to the table, drew his chair up, and helped himself to a large slice of cold pie.

Toad was quite alarmed at this very serious style of greeting; but the Rat whispered to him, 'Never mind, don't take any notice; and don't say anything to him just yet. He's always rather low when he's hungry. In half an hour's time he'll be quite a different animal.'

So they waited in silence, and presently there came another and a lighter knock. The Rat, with a nod to Toad, went to the door and ushered in the Mole, very shabby and unwashed, with bits of hay and straw sticking in his fur.

'Hooray! Here's old Toad!' cried the Mole, his face beaming. 'Fancy having you back again!' And he began to dance round him. 'We never dreamt you would turn up so soon! Why, you must have managed to escape, you clever Toad!'

The Rat; alarmed, pulled him by the elbow; but it was too late. Toad was puffing and swelling already.

'Clever? O no!' he said. 'I'm not really clever, according to my friends. I've only broken out of the strongest prison in England, that's all! And captured a railway train and escaped on it, that's all! And disguised myself and gone about the country tricking everybody, that's all! O no! I'm a stupid fool, I am! I'll tell you one or two of my little adventures, Mole, and you shall judge for yourself!'

'Well, well,' said the Mole, moving towards the supper table, 'supposing you talk while I eat. Not a bite since breakfast! O my! O my!' And he sat down and helped himself to cold beef and pickles.

Toad stood, legs apart, on the hearth-rug, thrust his paw into his trouser-pocket and pulled out a handful of silver. 'Look at that!' he cried, displaying it. 'That's not so bad, is it, for a few minutes' work? And how do you think I done it, Mole? Horse-stealing! That's how I done it!'

'Go on, Toad,' said the Mole, immensely interested.

'Toad, do be quiet, please!' said the Rat. 'And don't you egg him on, Mole, when you know what he is; but please tell us as soon as possible what the position is, and what's best to be done, now that Toad is back at last.'

'The position's about as bad as it can be,' replied the Mole grumpily, 'and as for what's to be done, why, blessed if I know! The Badger and I have been round and round the place, by night and by day; always the same thing. Sentries posted everywhere, guns poked out at us, stones thrown at us; always an animal on the look-out, and when they see us, my, how they do laugh! That's what annoys me most!'

'It's a very difficult situation,' said the Rat, reflecting deeply. 'But I think I see now, in the depths of my mind, what Toad really ought to do. I will tell you. He ought to—'

'No, he oughtn't!' shouted the Mole, with his mouth full. 'Nothing of the sort! You don't understand. What he ought to do is, he ought to —'

'Well, I shan't do it, anyway!' cried Toad, getting excited. 'I'm not going to be ordered about by you fellows! It's *my* house we're talking about, and *I* know exactly what to do, and I'll tell you. I'm going to —'

By this time they were all three talking at once, at the top of their voices, and the noise was simply deafening, when a thin, dry voice made itself heard, saying, 'Be quiet at once, all of you!' and instantly everyone was silent.

It was the Badger, who, having finished his pie, had turned round in his chair and was looking at them severely.

'Toad! ' he said. 'You bad, troublesome little animal! Aren't you ashamed of yourself? What do you think your father, my old friend, would have said if he had been here tonight, and had known of all your goings on?'

Toad, who was on the sofa by this time, with his legs up, rolled over on his face, shaken by sobs of regret.

'There, there!' went on the Badger more kindly. 'Never mind. Stop crying. We're going to let bygones be bygones, and try and turn over a new leaf. But what the Mole says is quite true. The stoats are on guard, at every point, and they make the best guards in the world. It's quite useless to think of attacking the place. They're too strong for us.'

'Then it's all over,' sobbed the Toad, crying into the sofa cushions. 'I shall go and enlist for a soldier, and never see my dear Toad Hall any more!'

'Come, cheer up, Toady!' said the Badger. 'There are more ways of getting back a place than taking it by storm. I haven't said my last word yet. Now I'm going to tell you a great secret.'

Toad sat up slowly and dried his eyes.

'There is an underground passage,' said the Badger impressively, 'that leads from the river bank quite near here, right up into the middle of Toad Hall.'

'O, nonsense, Badger!' said Toad rather airily. 'You've been listening to some of the yarns they spin in the public houses about here. I know every inch of Toad Hall, inside and out. Nothing of the sort, I do assure you!'

'My young friend,' said the Badger with great severity, 'your father, who was a worthy animal, a lot worthier than some others I know, was a particular friend of mine, and told me a great deal he wouldn't have dreamt of telling you. He discovered that passage. He didn't make it, of course; that was done hundreds of years before he ever came to live there, and he repaired it and cleaned it out, because he thought it might come in useful some day, in case of trouble or danger; and he showed it to me. "Don't let my son know about it," he said. "He's a good boy, but very light and unstable in character, and simply cannot hold his tongue. If he's ever in a real fix, and it would be of use to him, you

may tell him about the secret passage; but not before."'

The other animals looked hard at Toad to see how he would take it. Toad was inclined to be sulky at first; but he brightened up immediately, like the good fellow he was.

'Well, well,' he said, 'perhaps I am a bit of a talker. A popular fellow such as I am, my friends get round me, we sparkle, we tell witty stories and somehow my tongue gets wagging. Go on, Badger. How's this passage of yours going to help us?'

'I've found out a thing or two lately,' continued the Badger. 'I got Otter to disguise himself as a sweep and call at the back door with brushes over his shoulder, asking for a job. There's going to be a big banquet tomorrow night. It's somebody's birthday, the Chief Weasel's, I believe, and all the weasels will be gathered together in the dining hall, eating and drinking and laughing and carrying on, suspecting nothing. No guns, no swords, no sticks, no arms of any sort whatever!'

'But the guards will be posted as usual,' remarked the Rat.

'Exactly,' said the Badger; 'that is my point. The weasels will trust entirely to their excellent guards. And that is where the passage comes in. That very useful tunnel leads right up under the butler's pantry, next to the dining hall!'

'Aha! That squeaky board in the butler's pantry!' said Toad. 'Now I understand it!'

'We shall creep out quietly into the butler's pantry!' cried the Mole.

'With our pistols and swords and sticks!' shouted the Rat.

'And rush in upon them!' said the Badger.

'And whack 'em, and whack 'em, and whack 'em!' cried the Toad, running round and round the room, and jumping over the chairs.

'Very well, then,' said the Badger, resuming his usual dry manner, 'our plan is settled. So, as it's getting very late, all of you go right off to bed at once. We will make all the necessary arrangements in the course of the morning tomorrow.'

Toad, of course, went off to bed dutifully with the rest, he knew better than to refuse, though he was feeling much too excited to sleep. But he had

had a long day, with many events crowded into it; and sheets and blankets were very friendly and comforting things, after plain straw, and not too much of it, spread on the stone floor of a draughty cell; and his head had not been many seconds on his pillow before he was snoring happily.

He slept till a late hour next morning, and by the time he got down he found that the other animals had finished their breakfast some time before. The Mole had slipped off somewhere by himself, without telling anyone where he was going. The Badger sat in the armchair, reading the paper, and not concerning himself in the slightest about what was going to happen that very evening. The Rat, on the other hand, was running round the room busily, with his arms full of weapons of every kind, distributing them in four little heaps on the floor, and saying excitedly under his breath, as he ran, 'Here's a sword for the Rat, here's a sword for the Mole, here's a sword for the Toad, here's a sword for the Badger! Here's a pistol for the Rat, here's a pistol for the Mole, here's a pistol for the Toad, here's a pistol for the Badger!'

And so on, while the four little heaps gradually grew and grew.

'That's all very well, Rat,' said the Badger presently, looking at the busy little animal over the edge of his newspaper. 'I'm not

blaming you. But just let us once get past the stoats, with those detestable guns of theirs, and I assure you we shan't want any swords or pistols. We four, with our sticks, once we're inside the dining hall, why, we shall clear the floor of all the lot of them in five minutes. I'd have done the whole thing by myself, only I didn't want to deprive you fellows of the fun!'

'It's as well to be on the safe side,' said the Rat reflectively, polishing a pistol barrel on his sleeve and looking along it.

The Toad, having finished his breakfast, picked up a stout stick and swung it vigorously, flattening imaginary animals.

Presently the Mole came tumbling into the room, evidently very pleased with himself. 'I've been having such fun!' he began at once. 'I've been getting a laugh out of the stoats!'

'I hope you've been very careful, Mole,' said the Rat anxiously.

'I should hope so, too,' said the Mole confidently. 'I got the idea when I went into the kitchen, to see about Toad's breakfast being kept hot for him. I found that old washerwoman dress that he came home in yesterday, hanging on a towel-horse before the fire. So I put it on, and the bonnet as well, and the shawl, and off I went to Toad Hall, as bold as you please. The sentries were on the look-out, of course, with their guns and their "Who comes there?" and all the rest of their nonsense. "Good morning, gentlemen!" says I, very respectful. "Want any washing done today?"

'They looked at me very proud and stiff and haughty, and said, "Go away, washerwoman! We don't do any washing on duty." "Or any other time?" says I. Ho, ho, ho! Wasn't I *funny*, Toad?'

'Poor, frivolous animal!' said Toad very loftily. The fact is, he felt exceedingly jealous of Mole for what he had just done. It was exactly what he would have liked to have done himself, if only he had thought of it first, and hadn't gone and overslept.

'Some of the stoats turned quite pink,' continued the Mole, 'and the sergeant in charge, he said to me, very short, he said, "Now run away, my good woman, run away! Don't keep my men idling and talking on their posts." "Run away?" says I. "It won't be me that'll be running away, in a very

short time from now!"'

'O, *Moley*, how could you?' said the Rat, dismayed.

The Badger laid down his paper.

'I could see them pricking up their ears and looking at each other,' went on the Mole 'and the sergeant said to them, "Never mind *her*; she doesn't know what she's talking about." "O! Don't I?" said I. "Well, let me tell you this. My daughter, she washes for Mr Badger, and that'll show you whether I know what I'm talking about; and *you'll* know pretty soon, too! A hundred bloodthirsty badgers, armed with rifles, are going to attack Toad Hall this very night, by way of the paddock. Six boat-loads of rats with pistols and cutlasses will come up the river and land in the garden; while a picked body of toads, known as the Die-hards, or the Death-or-Glory Toads, will storm the orchard and carry everything before them, yelling for vengeance. There won't be much left of you to wash, by the time they've done with you, unless you clear out while you have the chance!"

'Then I ran away, and when I was out of sight I hid; and presently I came creeping back along the ditch and took a peep at them through the hedge. They were all as nervous and flustered as could be, running all ways at once, and falling

...140...

over each other, and everyone giving orders to everybody else and not listening; and the sergeant kept sending off parties of stoats to distant parts of the grounds, and then sending other fellows to fetch 'em back again: and I heard them saying to each other, "That's *just* like the weasels; they're to stop comfortably in the banqueting hall, and have feasting and toasts and songs and all sorts of fun, while we must stay on guard in the cold and the dark, and in the end be cut to pieces by bloodthirsty Badgers!"'

'O, you silly fool, Mole!' cried Toad. 'You've been and spoilt everything!'

'Mole,' said the Badger, in his dry, quiet way, 'I can see you have more sense in your little finger than some other animals have in the whole of their fat bodies. You have managed excellently, and I begin to have great hopes of you. Good Mole! Clever Mole!'

The Toad was simply wild with jealousy, more especially as he couldn't make out for the life of him what the Mole had done that was so particularly clever; but, fortunately for him, before he could show temper or expose himself to the Badger's sarcasm, the bell rang for lunch.

It was a simple meal, bacon and broad beans, and a macaroni pudding; and when they had quite done, the Badger settled himself into an armchair, and said, 'Well, we've got our work cut out for us tonight, and it will probably be pretty late before we're quite through with it; so I'm just going to take forty winks, while I can.' And he drew a handkerchief over his face and was soon snoring.

The hard-working Rat at once resumed his preparations, and started running between his four little heaps, muttering, 'Here's a belt for the Rat, here's a belt for the Mole, here's a belt for the Toad, here's a belt for the Badger!' and so on, with every fresh item he produced, to which there seemed really no end; so the Mole drew his arm through Toad's, led him out into the open air, shoved him into a wicker chair, and made him tell him all his adventures from beginning to end, which Toad was only too willing to do. The Mole was a good listener, and Toad, with no one to check his statements or to criticise in an unfriendly spirit, rather let himself go. Indeed, much that he related belonged more properly to the category of what-might-have-happened-had-I-only-thought-of-it-in-time-instead-of-ten-minutes-afterwards. Those are always the best adventures; and why should they not be truly ours, as much as the somewhat inadequate things that really come off?

CHAPTER 10

The Return of The Hero

WHEN it began to grow dark, the Rat, with an air
of excitement and mystery, called them back into the
parlour, stood each of them up alongside his little heap,
and proceeded to dress them up for the coming expedition.
He was very earnest and thorough going about it, and the
affair took quite a long time. First, there was a belt to go
round each animal, and then a sword to be stuck into each
belt, and then a cutlass on the other side to balance it. Then
a pair of pistols, a policeman's truncheon, several sets of
handcuffs, some bandages and sticking-plaster, and a flask
and a sandwich-case. The Badger laughed and said, 'All right,
Ratty! It amuses you and it doesn't hurt me. I'm going to do
all I've got to do with this here stick.' But the Rat only said,
'*Please*, Badger! You know I shouldn't like you to blame me

afterwards and say I had forgotten *anything*!'

When all was quite ready, the Badger took a dark lantern in one paw, grasped his great stick with the other, and said, 'Now then, follow me! Mole first, 'cos I'm very pleased with him; Rat next; Toad last. And look here, Toady! Don't you chatter so much as usual, or you'll be sent back, as sure as fate!'

The Toad was so anxious not to be left out that he took up the lowly position given to him without a murmur, and the animals set off. The Badger led them along by the river for a little way, and then suddenly swung himself over the edge into a hole in the river bank, a little above the water. The Mole and the Rat followed silently, swinging themselves successfully into the hole as they had seen the Badger do; but when it came to Toad's turn, of course he managed to slip and fall into the water with a loud splash and a squeal of alarm. He was hauled out by his friends, rubbed down and wrung out hastily, comforted, and set on his legs; but the Badger was angry, and told him that the very next time he made a fool of himself he would most certainly be left behind.

So at last they were in the secret passage, and the driving out expedition had really begun!

It was cold, and dark, and damp, and low, and narrow, and poor Toad began to shiver, partly from dread of what might be before him, partly because he was wet through. The lantern was far ahead, and he could not help lagging behind a little in the darkness. Then he heard the Rat call out warningly, '*Come* on, Toad!' and a terror seized him of being left behind, alone in the darkness, and he 'came on' with such a rush that he upset the Rat into the Mole and the Mole into the Badger, and for a moment all was confusion. The Badger thought they were being attacked from behind, and, as there was no room to use a stick or a cutlass, drew a pistol, and was on the point of putting a bullet into Toad. When he found out what had really happened he was very angry indeed, and said, 'Now this time that tiresome Toad *shall* be left behind!'

But Toad whimpered, and the other two promised that they would be answerable for his good conduct, and at last the Badger was pacified, and the procession moved on; only this time the Rat brought up the rear, with a firm grip on the shoulder of Toad.

So they groped and shuffled along, with their ears pricked up and their paws on their pistols, till at last the Badger said, 'We ought by now to be pretty nearly under the Hall.'

Then suddenly they heard, far away as it might be, and yet nearly over their heads, a confused murmur of sound, as if people were shouting and cheering and stamping on the floor and hammering on tables. The Toad's nervous terrors all returned, but the Badger only remarked placidly, 'They *are* going it, the weasels!'

The passage now began to slope upwards; they groped onward a little further, and then the noise broke out again, quite distinct this time, and very close above them. 'Ooo-ray-oo-ray-oo-ray-ooray!' they heard, and the stamping of little feet on the floor, and the clinking of glasses as little fists pounded on the table. '*What* a time they're having!' said the Badger. 'Come on!' They hurried along the passage till it came to a full stop, and they found themselves standing under the trapdoor that led up into the butler's pantry.

Such a tremendous noise was going

on in the banqueting hall that there was little danger of their being overheard. The Badger said, 'Now, boys, all together!' and the four of them put their shoulders to the trapdoor and heaved it back. Hoisting each other up, they found themselves standing in the pantry, with only a door between them and the banqueting hall, where their enemies were making merry.

The noise, as they emerged from the passage, was simply deafening. At last, as the cheering and hammering slowly subsided, a voice could be made out saying, 'Well, I do not propose to detain you much longer' (great applause) 'but before I resume my seat' (renewed cheering) 'I should like to say one word about our kind host, Mr Toad. We all know Toad!' (great laughter) '*Good* Toad, *modest* Toad, *honest* Toad!' (shrieks of merriment).

'Only just let me get at him!' muttered Toad, grinding his teeth.

'Hold hard a minute!' said the Badger, restraining him with difficulty. 'Get ready, all of you!'

'Let me sing you a little song,' went on the voice, 'which I have composed on the subject of Toad'

(prolonged applause).

Then the Chief Weasel, for it was he, began in a high, squeaky voice: 'Toad he went a-pleasuring gaily down the street –'

The Badger drew himself up, took a firm grip of his stick with both paws, glanced round at his comrades, and cried:

'The hour is come! Follow me!'

And flung the door open wide.

My!

What a squealing and a squeaking and a screeching filled the air!

Well might the terrified weasels dive under the tables and spring madly up at the windows! Well might the ferrets rush wildly for the fireplace and get hopelessly jammed in the chimney! Well might tables and chairs be upset, and glass and china be sent crashing on the floor, in the panic of that terrible moment when the four Heroes strode wrathfully into the room! The mighty Badger, his whiskers bristling, his great cudgel whistling through the air; Mole, black and grim, brandishing his stick and shouting his awful war-cry, 'A Mole! A Mole!' Rat, desperate and determined, his belt bulging with weapons of every age and every variety; Toad, frenzied with excitement and injured pride, swollen to twice his ordinary size, leaping into the air and crying out Toad-whoops that chilled them to the marrow! 'Toad he went a-pleasuring!' he yelled. 'I'll pleasure 'em!' and he went straight for the Chief Weasel. They were but four in all, but to the panic-stricken weasels the hall seemed full of monstrous animals, grey, black, brown, and yellow, whooping and flourishing enormous cudgels; and they broke and fled with squeals of terror and dismay, this way and that, through the windows, up the chimney, anywhere to get out of reach of those terrible sticks.

The affair was soon over. Up and down, the whole length of the hall, strode the four friends, whacking with their sticks at every head that showed itself; and in five minutes the room was cleared. Through the broken windows the shrieks of terrified weasels escaping across the lawn were borne faintly to their ears; on the floor lay some dozen or so of the enemy, on whom the Mole was busily engaged in fitting handcuffs. The Badger, resting from his labours, leant on his stick and wiped his honest brow.

'Mole,' he said, 'you're the best of fellows! Just cut along outside and look after those stoat-sentries of yours, and see what they're doing. I've an idea that, thanks to you, we shan't have much trouble from *them* tonight!'

The Mole vanished promptly through a window; and the Badger got the other two to set a table on its legs again, pick up knives and forks and plates and glasses from the muddle on the floor, and see if they could find materials for a supper. 'I want some grub, I do,' he said, in that rather common way he had of speaking. 'Stir your stumps, Toad, and look lively! We've got your house back for you, and you don't offer us so much as a sandwich.'

Toad felt rather hurt that the Badger didn't say pleasant things to him, as he had to the Mole, and tell him what a fine fellow he was, and how splendidly he had fought; for he

was rather particularly pleased with himself and the way he had gone for the Chief Weasel and sent him flying across the table with one blow of his stick. But he bustled about, and so did the Rat, and soon they found a cold chicken, a tongue that had hardly been touched, some trifle, and quite a lot of lobster salad; and in the pantry they came upon a basketful of French rolls and any quantity of cheese, butter, and celery. They were just about to sit down when the Mole clambered in through the window, chuckling, with an armful of rifles.

'It's all over,' he reported. 'From what I can make out, as soon as the stoats, who were very nervous and jumpy already, heard the shrieks and the yells and the uproar inside the hall, some of them threw down their rifles and fled. The others stood fast for a bit, but when the weasels came rushing out upon them they thought they were betrayed; and the stoats grappled with the weasels, and the weasels fought to get away, and they wrestled and wriggled and punched each other, and rolled over and over, till most of 'em rolled into the river! They've all disappeared by now, one way or another; and I've got their rifles. So *that's* all right!'

'Excellent and deserving animal!' said the Badger, his mouth full of chicken and trifle. 'Now, there's just one more thing I want you to do, Mole, before you sit down to your supper with us; and I wouldn't trouble you only I know I can trust you to see a thing done, and I wish I could say the same of everyone I know. I'd send Rat, if he wasn't a poet. I want you to take those fellows on the floor there upstairs with you, and have some bedrooms cleaned out and tidied up and made really comfortable. See that they sweep *under* the beds, and put clean sheets and pillowcases on, and turn down one corner

of the bedclothes, just as you know it ought to be done; and have a can of hot water, and clean towels, and fresh cakes of soap put in each room. And then you can give them a licking, if it's any satisfaction to you, and put them out by the back door, and we shan't see any more of *them*, I fancy. And then come along and have some of this cold tongue. It's first-rate. I'm very pleased with you, Mole!'

The good-natured Mole picked up a stick, formed his prisoners up in a line on the floor, gave them the order 'Quick march!' and led his squad off to the upper floor. After a time, he appeared again, smiling, and said that every room was ready, and as clean as a new pin. 'And I didn't have to lick them, either,' he added. 'I thought, on the whole, they had had licking enough for one night, and the weasels, when I put the point to them, quite agreed with me, and said they wouldn't think of troubling me. They said they were extremely sorry for what they had done, but it was all the fault of the Chief Weasel and the stoats, and if ever they could do anything for us at any time to make up, we had only got to mention it. So I gave them a roll each, and let them out at the back, and off they ran, as hard as they could!'

Then the Mole pulled his chair up to the table, and pitched into the cold tongue; and Toad, like the gentleman he was, put all his jealousy from him, and said heartily, 'Thank you kindly, dear Mole, for all your pains and trouble tonight, and especially for your cleverness this morning!' The Badger was pleased at that, and said, 'There spoke my brave Toad!' So they finished their supper in great joy and contentment, and presently retired to rest between clean sheets, safe in Toad's ancestral home, won

back by great courage, perfect strategy, and a proper handling of sticks.

The following morning, Toad, who had overslept as usual, came down to breakfast disgracefully late, and found on the table a certain quantity of egg shells, some fragments of cold and leathery toast, a coffee pot three-quarters empty, and really very little else; which did not tend to improve his temper, considering that, after all, it was his own house. Through the French windows of the breakfast-room he could see the Mole and the Water Rat sitting in wicker chairs out on the lawn, evidently telling each other stories; roaring with laughter and kicking their short legs up in the air. The Badger, who was in an armchair and deep in the morning paper, merely looked up and nodded when Toad entered the room. So Toad sat down and made the best breakfast he could, merely observing to himself that he would get square with the others sooner or later. When he had nearly finished, the Badger looked up and remarked rather shortly: 'I'm sorry, Toad, but I'm afraid there's a heavy morning's work in front of you. You see, we really ought to have a banquet at once, to celebrate this affair. It's expected of you: in fact, it's the rule.'

'O, all right!' said the Toad readily. 'Anything to oblige. Though why on earth you should want to have a banquet in the morning I cannot understand. But you know I do not live to please myself, but merely to find out what my friends want, and then try and arrange it for 'em, you dear old Badger!'

'Don't pretend to be more stupid than you really are,' replied the Badger crossly, 'and don't chuckle and splutter in your coffee while you're talking; it's not manners. What I mean is, the banquet will be at night, of course, but the invitations will have to be written and got off at once, and you've got to write 'em. Now, sit down at that table, there's stacks of letter-paper on it, with "Toad Hall" at the top in blue and gold, and write invitations to all our friends, and if you stick to it we shall get them out before lunch. And *I'll* lend a hand, too, and take my share of the burden. *I'll* order the Banquet.'

'What?' cried Toad, dismayed. 'Me stop indoors and write a lot of rotten letters on a fine morning like this, when I want to go around my property, and set everything and everybody to rights, and swagger about and enjoy myself? Certainly not! I'll be – I'll see you – stop a minute, though! Why, of course, dear Badger! What is my pleasure or convenience compared with that of others? You wish it done, and it shall be done. Go, Badger, order the Banquet, order what you like; then join our young friends outside, forget about me and my cares and toils. I sacrifice this fair morning to duty

and friendship!'

The Badger looked at him very suspiciously, but Toad's frank, open face made it difficult to suggest any unworthy motive in this change of attitude. He left the room in the direction of the kitchen, and as soon as the door had closed behind him, Toad hurried to the writing table. A fine idea had occurred to him while he was talking. He *would* write the invitations; and he would take care to mention the leading part he had taken in the fight, and how he had laid the Chief Weasel flat; and he would hint at his adventures, and what a career of triumph he had to tell about; and on the first page he would give a sort of programme of entertainment for the evening, something like this, as he sketched it out in his head:

SPEECH BY TOAD
(There will be other speeches by Toad during the evening)

ADDRESS BY TOAD
Synopsis – Our Prison System – The Waterways of Old England –
Horse-dealing and How to Deal – Property, Its Rights and Its Duties –
Back to the Land – A Typical English Squire

SONG BY TOAD
(Composed by himself)

OTHER COMPOSITIONS BY TOAD
will be sung in the course of the evening by the
COMPOSER

The idea pleased him mightily, and he worked very hard and got all the letters finished by noon, at which hour it was reported to him that there was a small and rather bedraggled weasel at the door, asking timidly whether he could be of any service to

the gentlemen. Toad swaggered out and found it was one of the prisoners of the previous evening, very respectful and eager to please. He patted him on the head, shoved the bundle of invitations into his paw, and told him to go along quickly and deliver them as fast as he could, and if he liked to come back again in the evening perhaps there might be a shilling for him, or, again, perhaps there mightn't; and the poor weasel seemed really quite grateful, and hurried off eagerly to do his mission.

When the other animals came back to lunch after a morning on the river, the Mole, feeling somewhat guilty, looked doubtfully at Toad, expecting to find him sulky or depressed. Instead, he was so uppish and inflated that the Mole began to suspect something; while the Rat and the Badger exchanged knowing glances.

As soon as the meal was over, Toad thrust his paws deep into his trouser pockets, remarked casually, 'Well, look after yourselves, you fellows! Ask for anything you want!' and was swaggering off in the direction of the garden where he wanted to think out an idea or two for his coming speeches, when the Rat caught him by the arm.

Toad rather suspected what he was after, and did his best to get away; but when the Badger took him firmly by the other arm he began to see that the game was up. The two animals took him between them into the small smoking room that opened out of the entrance hall, shut the door, and put him into a chair.

'Now, look here, Toad,' said the Rat. 'It's about this banquet, and very sorry I am to have to speak to you like this. But we want you to understand

clearly, once and for all, that there are going to be no speeches and no songs. Try and grasp the fact that on this occasion we're not arguing with you; we're just telling you.'

Toad saw that he was trapped. They understood him, they saw through him, they had got ahead of him. His pleasant dream was shattered.

'Can't I sing them just one *little* song?' he pleaded.

'No, not *one* little song,' replied the Rat firmly, though his heart bled as he noticed the trembling lip of the poor Toad. 'It's no good, Toady; you know well that your songs are all conceit and boasting and vanity; and your speeches are all self-praise and - and - well, and gross exaggeration and, – and –'

'And gas,' put in the Badger, in his common way.

'It's for your own good, Toady,' went on the Rat. 'You know you *must* turn over a new leaf sooner or later, and now seems a splendid time to begin; a sort of turning point in your career. Please don't think that saying all this doesn't hurt me more than it hurts you.'

Toad remained a long while plunged in thought. At last he raised his head, and the traces of strong emotion could be seen on his face. 'You have conquered, my friends,' he said sadly. 'It was, to be sure, but a small thing that I asked just to expand for yet one more evening, to let myself go and hear the deafening applause that always seems to me, somehow, to bring out my best qualities. However, you are right, and I am wrong. From now on I will be a very different Toad. My friends, you shall never have to blush for me again. But, O dear, O dear this is a hard world!'

And, pressing his handkerchief to his face, he left the room with faltering footsteps.

'Badger,' said the Rat, 'I feel like a brute; I wonder what *you* feel like?'

'O, I know, I know,' said the Badger gloomily. 'But the thing had to be done. This good fellow has got to live here, and hold his own, and be respected. Would you have him a common laughing stock, mocked and jeered at by stoats and weasels?'

'Of course not,' said the Rat. 'And, talking of weasels, it's lucky we came upon that little weasel, just as he was setting out with Toad's invitations. I suspected something from what you told me, and had a look at one or two; they were simply disgraceful. I did away with the lot, and the good Mole is now sitting in the blue *boudoir*, filling up plain, simple invitation cards.'

At last the hour for the banquet began to draw near, and Toad, who on leaving the others had retired to his bedroom, was still sitting there, sad and thoughtful. His brow resting on his paw, he pondered long and deeply. Gradually his face cleared, and he began to smile long, slow smiles. Then he took to giggling in a

shy, self-conscious manner. At last he got up, locked the door, drew the curtains across the windows, collected all the chairs in the room and arranged them in a semicircle, and took up his position in front of them, swelling visibly. Then he bowed, coughed twice, and, letting himself go, with uplifted voice he sang, to the enraptured audience that his imagination so clearly saw,

TOAD'S LAST LITTLE SONG!

The Toad came home!
There was panic in the parlour and howling in the hall,
There was crying in the cow-shed and shrieking in the stall,
When the Toad came home!
When the Toad came home!
There was smashing in of window and crashing in of door,
There was chivvying of weasels that fainted on the floor,
When the Toad came home!

Bang! go the drums!
The trumpeters are tooting and the soldiers are saluting,
And the cannon they are shooting and the motor-cars are hooting,
As the Hero comes!

Shout *Hooray!*
And let each one of the crowd try and shout it very loud,
In honour of an animal of whom you're justly proud,
For it's Toad's great day!

He sang this very loudly, with great energy and expression; and when he had done, he sang it all over again.

Then he heaved a deep sigh; a long, long, long sigh.

Then he unlocked the door and went quietly down the stairs to greet his guests, who he knew must be assembling in the drawing room.

All the animals cheered when he entered, and crowded round to congratulate him and say nice things about his courage, and his cleverness, and his fighting qualities; but Toad only smiled faintly and murmured, 'Not at all!' Or, sometimes, for a change, 'On the contrary!' Otter, who was standing on the hearth rug, describing to an admiring circle of friends exactly how he would have managed things had he been there, came forward with a shout, threw his arm round Toad's neck, and tried to take him round the room in triumphal progress; but Toad, in a mild way, was rather snubby to him, remarking gently, as he disengaged himself, 'Badger was the mastermind; the Mole and the Water Rat bore the brunt of the fighting; I merely served in the ranks and did little or nothing.' The animals were evidently puzzled and taken aback by this unexpected attitude of his; and Toad felt, as he moved from one guest to the other, making his modest responses, that he was an object of great interest to everyone.

The Badger had ordered everything of the best, and the banquet was a great success. There was much talking and laughter among the animals, but through it all Toad looked down his nose and murmured pleasant nothings to the animals on either side of him. Now and then he stole a glance at the Badger and the Rat, and always when he looked they were staring at each other with their mouths open; and this gave him the greatest satisfaction. Some of the younger and livelier animals, as the evening wore on, got whispering to each other that things were not so amusing as they used to be in the good old days; and there were some knockings on the table and cries of 'Toad! Speech! Speech from Toad! Song! Mr Toad's Song!' But Toad only shook his head gently, raised one paw in mild protest, and managed to convey to them that this dinner was being run on strictly conventional lines. He was indeed an altered Toad!

* * * * * * * * * * * *

After this climax, the four animals continued to lead their lives, so rudely broken in upon by civil war, in great joy and contentment, undisturbed by further risings or invasions.

Toad, after due consultation with his friends, selected a handsome gold chain and locket set with pearls, which he dispatched to the jailer's daughter with a letter that even the Badger admitted to be modest and grateful. The engine driver, in his turn, was properly thanked and rewarded for all his pains and trouble. Under the strongest pressure from the Badger, even the barge woman was, with some trouble, sought out and the value of her horse made good to her; though Toad kicked terribly at this, holding himself to be an instrument of Fate, sent to punish fat women with mottled arms who couldn't tell a real gentleman when they saw one. The amount involved, it was true, was not very great. Local traders agreed that the price the gipsy had paid was approximately correct.

Sometimes, in the course of long summer evenings, the friends would take a stroll together in the Wild Wood, now successfully tamed so far as

they were concerned; and it was pleasing to see how respectfully they were greeted by the inhabitants, and how the mother-weasels would bring their young ones to the mouths of their holes, and say, pointing, 'Look, baby! There goes the great Mr Toad! And that's the gallant Water Rat, a terrible fighter, walking along with him! And yonder comes the famous Mr Mole, of whom you so often have heard your father tell!' But when their infants were troublesome and quite beyond control, they would quiet them by telling how, if they didn't hush and not fret them, the terrible grey Badger would up and get them. This was not true at all of Badger, who, though he cared little about Society, was rather fond of children; but it never failed to have its full effect.